THE
CHICAGO
EAST INDIA
COMPANY

THE CHICAGO EAST INDIA COMPANY

CHRISTOPHER LYKE

DOUBLE‡DAGGER

Library and Archives Canada Cataloguing in Publication
Lyke, Christopher. author
The Chicago East India Company / Christopher Lyke

Issued in print and electronic formats.
ISBN: 978-1-990644-22-1 (soft cover)
ISBN: 978-1-990644-23-8 (e-book)

Editor: Phil Halton
Interior Design: Pablo Javier Herrera
Cover Design: Spencer Robens Designs

Double Dagger Books Ltd
Toronto, Ontario, Canada
www.doubledagger.ca

For E, C, & J

THE BIRDMAN OF BUCKTOWN

IF THE ROMANS HAD SETTLED THIS LAND instead of Enlightenment-era Brits we'd be worshiping Sol Invictus.

Every year the city dies a horrid, frozen death. And every year it comes slowly back to life. Road crews arrive with hot-patch and trucks to fix streets that are cracked and sinking under the weight of a thawing city. Parents breathe a sigh of relief as they no longer worry for tiny fingers that freeze in wet mittens. The dog moves off the heating vent, and fifty-five degrees feels like eighty-five as the young traipse from bar to bar in shorts and hoodies praising Sol without knowing it. It is spring, and it is bright, and in the evenings it is red. Maybe we'd have more fun if we still worshiped like that. At any rate, winter was gone and the city was rubbing itself up against the May sun.

It came through the car windows and living rooms and warmed the cat. Bushes were wild, and grass grew up through the cracked, shit asphalt in the alley. Trees loosed pollen that pooled up in the sidewalks and the corners of buildings. Pedallers streamed past in droves in the little bike lanes, all of them smug and young and sure of everything. They leave college and discover the city. They troupe through its jungles with pikes and steel helmets and presume to be the first to stay up till the birds start singing. They fuck and divine themselves through the same streets the older ones had, only now they're a mile northwest of where they used to be. The traveling circus moves down the CTA a couple stops and digs in. The pikes get set against the wall and bladed helmets become bassinets. Dollar stores become brunch places with one-word names that my parents wouldn't believe could charge so much for eggs and a beer for Sunday breakfast.

The wife and I are raising our kids here. We didn't decide so much as it just kind of happened. We let the city choose for us really. My kids go to school in the same neighborhood we'd become adults. It looks different now. Everyone that stayed and resisted the suburban yards had gotten better jobs and more expensive tastes. The dollar stores had mostly vanished. Yoga shops and expensive shoe stores sprang up all around the brunch factories and only the stalwart bars remained. The same doorman and bartender and record collection still reside at The Rainbo. All of us a bit older and a bit less on the prowl. The families that spoke Spanish moved west as the Germans and Norwegians and WASPs all moved back into the neighborhoods their forefathers had left in the early sixties. Such is the way of the city. It is never stagnant in those places and looks either like progress or oppression. It looks logical or unfair. All of it is true and untrue. The only certainty is that the city will winter, shed its leaves and begin growing anew, year after year. Chicago is a bully. Don't forget it. It's as natural as the prairie it stomped to death there on the shore of Lake Michigan. Crying about it does not help.

I spend most evenings in the summer on our tiny deck. It juts out from the second floor of our apartment and overlooks Armitage Avenue and the Santeria chicken shop that has held out for fifty years. Men in western gear show up at all hours and leave with the birds. A year ago, new-comer yuppies protested the place while we shouted at them to go home from our perch.

The wife and I sit out there and listen to music and drink beer and enjoy the seventy-degree evenings looking at the angels perched along the top of St. Mary's and the Hancock building in the distance. The cars rush by like the tide. It can put you to sleep. The sky from up there is open and has blues and pinks in the afternoon. There are purples and contrails in the evening. The kids play just inside the door while the wife and I cast spells and perfect stories.

I thought about Private Lunt recently. Jesus, it had been ten years. Ten years since coming home from Afghanistan jumpy and feral. Passing out on Division Street in the middle of the day. Trying to pass as a normal person on the train or picking up the kids at daycare. I thought about what happened to Lunt and some of the others. As time passes the edges soften and round. And everything that happened changes. We often view history through our lens now, instead of our lens then, when it mattered. When it could jump up and bite you. It's important not to be tricked by the time of softening hearts.

BURN PIT

THE TWO MEN HAD KNOWN EACH OTHER for exactly a week. They sat at a wooden table on the sidewalk near Third and Magazine and swapped jokes and carried on. The old jokes were new, and the laughter was loud and hollow. There were several drinks in front of them. They watched the old black man carve up oysters in front of the bar. He had a plastic table with a large wooden cutting board and a cooler full of fresh shellfish. His hands were rough and seemed to shake except for when he carved into the oyster. The new friends had already bought a dozen.

"You were a soldier. Tell me a war story," the older man said.

"I don't know, Tweedy."

The older man ignored him. "And not one you'd tell the wife. Tell me a real story."

His voice was southern and knuckle-balled and grew vines that curled for sunlight. It surrounded them. It wasn't nasal and sharp like the soldier's. It wasn't midwestern. It enveloped the space around them, and the soldier liked to hear it. He didn't want to tell a story though, the last time he told a war story was at a wedding and he'd been too drunk and told one and felt like vomiting in the morning for doing it. But Tweedy kept asking, and they kept drinking, and the sun was warm in March on the patio along Magazine street.

"Okay, writer-man, I'll tell you a real story."

"Excellent. Tell me how it felt. I want to feel it."

The burn pit bled down through the middle of the outpost. A wrinkle, that was all it was really, like a big ditch. But it was deep enough for a man to stand in and longer still. The outhouses were on one side of the vein, while the tents butt up against the mountain were on the other. There was a plank bridge at the narrowest part though one could jump it easily. The pit leaked down from where the half-cut drums taken from the backs of the outhouses were poured, pooling up as ash and rancid material in the deepest part of the trench. It was a pear, or a tear shape. Two young Pashai boys would come every day and burn the refuse from our bodies. They burned garbage too. Plastic. Old shirts. We called them names and threw things in their direction in the way that older brothers do. But that was a lie. One of them could have fallen in the pit and we wouldn't have cared. Not really.

The boys' boss was named Mohammed. He was the foreman for all the workers on our small outpost. We clung to the mountain along the river. The locals helped us build and dig. We used them for labor while we went out trying to find and hurt their cousins.

And we guarded the new, paved road that grew north from Mehtar Lam. It was our railroad. We guarded the valley passes near it. We protected it from the Indians. We invited commerce. We were rustbelt flatlanders and hillbillies from Georgia. We weren't used to the mountains. But everyone changes after a few weeks there. Your lungs change. Your legs change. They become hard. Most of us lost any fat after a month and belts became tight and armor wrapped around torsos that looked more like knots than some actors' pretty bodies.

Tribal tattoos and Viking ink peeked out from rolled up sleeves and the Nomex gloves with the hard knuckles. And if no one was trying to kill us it would have been a grand time. As it was, we had our quiet moments waiting for the sun to rise while on guard or listening to the river crash by in the spring. Perched above a town and dug in between the boulders, we watched and enjoyed the wind on our faces. We had our moments. We didn't trust any of it for very long.

Mohammed spent much of the autumn of '08 filming us from his stone hut across the river from the outpost. He had camera equipment set up on tripods back away from the window and in the middle of his one room hut. The window had two embroidered curtains that fluttered. We couldn't see the glint off the lens. It sat there filming us from across the river as we went about our daily routines. He filmed us filling generators. He filmed us in fights with the enemy. He filmed us changing guard rotations. He filmed us limping back from long patrols in the high ground. It always rolled, and he always gave the recordings to the enemy. And then he would walk across the wooden bridge over the river and on to our outpost to run the workers and take our money. He was good at this and we didn't realize he was a spy until he was gone. One day he just stopped coming. We never heard from him again. He'd been in trouble. His men were doing shoddy work and he was acting a bit too friendly with the people we already suspected. After too much complaining, and a couple rumors from a turncoat that liked heroin more than he liked the cause, Mohammed never came back. A couple days of absence and we crossed the wooden plank over the river and into his home in Dumlum. We found the cameras but not Mohammed.

The little boys came back. I forget their names. Maybe Shit and Fuck we called them. Something terrible anyway. They must have known all along. They came back, and no one said anything to them about the spy. They were just school aged boys from Dumlum. Maybe twelve years old. They smiled and played catch with us and bummed cigarettes. The captain said we needed to find Mohammed if we could. The shit boys said we'd never find him and that he was gone. But we looked anyway.

We woke and drove through the valleys on rock and earthen roads barely wider than our trucks. We'd dismount and climb up through towns peering in and around wooden doors and walled forts. We pointed weapons and grabbed men roughly. None of us looked at the women or else they'd get beaten. We always watched their hands though. We didn't find anything.

We hunted the Sioux and all the while the little boys dragged garbage and waste to the burn pit. It all went in there. They dumped diesel on the shit and stirred. They poured diesel over all the plastic water bottles and ripped clothes. They threw a match and it all would burn. They would do this, and we would get on with our business. We'd leave in the morning before dawn. Watch some village. Take someone's weapons. Give some hungry, scared people some trinkets and move along. We'd walk through the mountains, or along a road looking for bombs some asshole planted to try and kill us. We hiked through villages, up through mountains to waterfalls that fell from the rocks down to pools in the low ground. Women and children bathed and washed their robes. Purples and reds and yellows stitched with gold loops. They were shining, stinking people. And they had been bathing in this waterfall when the snow melted for hundreds of years. We'd watch and then head back home. Sometimes the other side would pick a fight, and sometimes he wouldn't. When we tried to pick one, they'd vanish, and we'd be left with jackals and porcupines and shale rock. They'd slip back into the terraced villages and would be gone.

The boys still came though. Every morning from across the river they came, checked in, and burned our shit. We played catch, and cracked wise, and laughed when they said dirty words in English. Eventually we headed up the Alishang valley towards the Dowlat Shah District Center. We entered the village at night and set up above it, out of sight. We'd gotten word that Mohammed was there, and we wanted them to wake up to thirty Americans in their town center. But as the sun rose, every chimney was pumping smoke down the valley telling everyone that we were there. And in the center of the village, across from a school our engineers had built, was Mohammed. He was laid out on his back and we could see his black hair and large nose from a hundred paces. We could see that it was him. His eyes were gone though, gouged or slashed out. And his throat cut and there were stab wounds of the worst kinds throughout his body. He wore white but that was dotted with deep awful red around the tears. One of his hands was missing fingers. It was the damndest thing. In the center of his chest was a dagger that pinned a piece of paper to his body. It was written in Pashai, I think, but could have been in Urdu. I couldn't have told you the difference.

In the end Mohammed couldn't win. I don't say this with remorse. I didn't care. None of us did, really. He'd filmed us and gauged us and helped their rockets land a bit truer. He'd alerted them by flashlight when we'd sneak out at night to some stone village or another. He wasn't our friend. Shit and Fuck didn't seem to care either. They were surprised that we'd been given the body. We gave the letter to our interpreter and intel guy and they passed it up the chain. It said everything you'd think it would and nothing at the same time. Declarations of war and what is godly were the big themes. Mostly it threatened those that dealt with the Americans. Even their own spies weren't safe. We laughed and made jokes about Mohammed with the boys. We taught them how to pretend to be dead with a tongue out and a hand holding an imaginary noose.

"Your story doesn't have a resolution." Tweedy said. He sold a lot of books and knew about these things.

"I know."

"Well, one has to have a resolution if you want the story to work."

"None of it ended. I thought about having one of the boys bring Mo's body in piece by piece to burn in the pit, but that would be false. There is no resolution. There was only the monotonous low-grade terror. And that pit constantly burning garbage and shit. Sometimes we'd try to kill each other but then it was back to silence. There was only the river rushing by. We went there, put our canoes in the water for a spell and then got out. Nothing changed."

"I see. Except for y'all. Some of you died and some of them died."

"Yeah. That's true." The soldier took a drink. "Those boys are probably eighteen or twenty now. About my daughter's age. They're probably dead or fighting."

"What are their odds?"

"Not good, Tweedy. Shit odds for sure."

"You're funny, soldier boy."

"Yeah. At least the Legions built their camps themselves when they were carving up the locals. I guess we were pretty trusting compared to those boys."

HUMBOLDT PARK

THE FOUR OF US LIVED at the corner of Hirsch and Maplewood. It wasn't the most dangerous part of the city in '97, but it wasn't out of the running either. Our landlady lived above us and tolerated our behavior mostly because her boyfriend was worse. He was ten years older than us and overweight but carried it well. His name was Shawn and he was a pretty rough around the edges white guy that rode his kid-sized BMX bike around the neighborhood doing tricks deep into his thirties. He had been a skateboarder in the early eighties and still liked the danger of flying over concrete. He wasn't bright, and I am pretty sure he was a heroin addict, and he was most certainly a burden to the landlady. One day when he was in the alley trying to jump his bike up a ramp onto the garage, he pissed off some Puerto Rican gangsters walking back from the corner store. They teased him and threw uncooked hot dogs at him until he went inside.

We usually ignored the gangsters. They happily called us neutrons and we were happy to be left alone. It wasn't until the police rounded up all the Puerto Ricans one weekend that we were messed with. The black gang moved in within a few hours and I was called "Fuck You, Richie Cunningham" by a young man who stood in the middle of the street in front of my beat-up van giving me the finger as I tried to leave. When the Puerto Ricans came back, it wasn't without a fight. They weren't throwing hot dogs then, and the police pulled us over on more than one occasion to ask us what the hell we were doing over so near to Humboldt Park.

The house next to ours was a typical three-flat occupied by one family. The matriarch lived on the first floor and her oldest son, Willie, acted like the cock of the walk. Willie was fortyish at the time. He seemed ancient. It was clear that he obeyed Mama though. There were other kids, including a younger man who was about our age. At one point this younger guy emptied his cheap pistol at a car that sped by our front door. He chased it down the street, shooting as he went. I don't know if it was related, but soon after that the cops found Willie shot to pieces in the alley a couple blocks away. He joined the wheelchaired ranks after that and someone built a ramp so that he could roll himself into the dilapidated three-flat and shit in a bag. There were other children, and grandchildren, but I could never keep track. They were almost always on the front stoop.

I didn't realize the basement of their house was a whorehouse until I moved into a room we used to store amplifiers. Four feet from my window, on the other side of the gangway, was a door that led to our neighbor's basement. It was a cheap plywood door about a quarter inch thick. I suspect it had a bathroom slide lock or a hook and loop lock on it to keep it shut most of the time. It banged open and shut most of the night during the summer and from it I could hear the drunks and the older scum bags breathing heavily and cruelly. I don't know who the girls were that Mama had working down there. I hope now that they weren't any part of her brood. Back then I didn't care. I didn't understand about children then.

One evening I heard a young woman crying. The head of my mattress was under the window. Mama was standing in the plywood doorway. I could have touched her if I leaned out of the window. The girl was crying that she didn't feel right and that she wasn't supposed to be like this. Mama was consoling her in a downhome, folksy kind of way. The girl continued and said that her Daddy would never have thought this would happen and that she wanted to stay pretty and to go home. Mama was silent for a minute and the girl pleaded with her again. I could hear myself breathe. Mama said, "Pretty's gotta bleed, girl." I heard the door close hard against the wooden frame and Mama shuffled off down the gangway to the back door.

I drive by the apartment every couple of months to see if much has changed. I keep hearing that Humboldt Park is less dangerous now, but I doubt it. There is still garbage in the little tree lawns between the sidewalk and the road and new condo buildings get tagged with gang symbols. The city sends out crews with power washers to blast the spray paint from the dark brick buildings, but it is hard to remove for good.

THE CHICAGO EAST INDIA COMPANY

ARTHUR BENNETT CALLED ME A RACIST. Well, it was implied. He was a black dude, sure, and the principal at Jackson Academy, yes, fine, but I wasn't a racist and he called me one. Fucking work.

"Why are all the black students sitting in one corner of your classroom and all the Latinos in the other?"

"Uh, I don't know Mr. Bennett. They're sitting with the people they want to sit with."

"Why would you do that?"

"Because they like getting to pick. I'm giving my students ownership."

He waved a long, skinny finger in my direction.

"No. No. No. No. No. No. No. This won't do. You're treating them differently and I want to know why!"

"Mr. Bennet, that's ridiculous. These kids love me. I'm not like that."

"Mr. Lyke." He paused. "Mr. Lyke." He paused again. "Mr. Lyke." Each time he said that, he kind of shook his head and closed his eyes and punctuated the last syllable by touching his finger to his thumb.

Bennet continued talking with his elbows on the desk in front of him. Behind him was a shelf with pristine copies of the Bhagavad-Gita and the Koran. He had books on slavery, teaching, Malcolm X, and a good-looking bible with gold leaf on the pages.

"What would you like me to do about the classroom? Move them all back to their old seats?"

"Yes, I would. Yes. Move them all back!"

"Okay."

"I won't have the brown kids marginalized, no sir." He waved a long finger in front of me again.

I'm sure the office girls heard him through the door. He was loud, and emphatic, and liked to pound on the desk. When he pulled a teacher into his office the girls spoke in hushed voices and put fingers to lips when anyone came in to ask for something.

"There's another thing." His eyes widened. "I heard you said something about the students to Doyle. Something about them being selfish, or how they can't learn." He paused. "He said you compared them to the Afghans."

Fucking Doyle.

"I can't keep you on if these things are true."

This was a lie. They could barely fire a teacher for fucking a student. And maybe not for punching one either. They usually pretended those things didn't happen. They usually searched for reasons to keep it out of the news while the offender sat at home collecting checks.

"No. It isn't true. I was just lamenting about how hard we try, and about how we're here for them, and they don't seem to care at all."

We continued talking, but immediately I knew this was a rookie mistake. It was the same feeling as passing out free supplies on patrol. I'd only been back in the States for about a year at that time, so it made sense that I'd conflate the two. Free beans and wind up radios. "Thank you, thank you. We're gonna try to kill you in about twenty minutes, but thanks for the free stuff." God dammit. It's frustrating. I'd been looking for a confidant and opened my damn mouth about it to Doyle. I had been trying to talk about the tricky quality of crusades. But all he heard was a coworker comparing students to boogeymen. I should have kept the conversation to the merits of Hunky Dory and OK Computer. My lens was curved differently from his and the way I saw things didn't make any sense to him. This kind of thing happened a lot at that school. And then at some point in the conversation I laughed at the students. It was too much for him, and as soon as I left the room, he ran to tell the boss. Or maybe he just liked to gossip and told the boss to gain some favor for himself. Anyway, that was the day before.

The whole thing is a gas really, it's a put on. The city wasn't honest about the schools. Not about these schools anyway. At least the Afghans were scared of us when we were trying to be nice. At least they didn't confuse it all.

Scared is useful. Scared can be enough. Being fed and clothed and paid makes arrangements happen. Who cares about being nice? It doesn't mean anything when you have total control over someone. With that kind of power, nice makes it worse. But scared counts. It gets the local bossman to send his young men to work at the outpost. It gets them to smile and talk about where bombs are planted in the road. They'll grin and ask for cigarettes. They'll bring stacks of flatbread. They'll even sidle up next to you and shoot their own countrymen. That's goddamn invaluable.

Save nice for the park league soccer coach. Jesus. Bennett and I were having a conversation about something I'd thought about for a long time but comparing it to teaching wasn't making any sense.

Maybe I didn't have the words anyway. I certainly didn't want to talk about race. At least not directly. He'd damn sure thought about that for a long time though. I'm sure he had something figured out too. He was smart, and he was pushing fifty at the time.

I tried to talk about humanity. I was poetic. I talked about how we were creatures brought to life from parts of the dead. I tried explaining that we were all great and awful and beautiful, and that we were all evil, too. We split the atom. We built Constantinople. We defied gravity. We were together, and we were there, working for Chicago Public Schools. I thought he'd understand when I said something less than the tagline, something that nobody at my last job would've considered troubling, that I didn't really mean it. Or, that no matter what I said I would still always do my best. We bitched a ton in the grunts, but we always got it done. Bennett listened with his face, but when I got going, I watched his eyes drift off to later in the day. They only came back when he could hear my cadence winding up.

I tried to talk to him about his books and about slavery and the Byzantines. He told me that was the wrong kind of slavery for us to worry about. So, I weaved in my time in Africa and the little village on the Somali border. Oh Gode! with the crocodiles and the dead hulks of generators sent in the 80s. Tombstone computers from Bob Geldoff and We Are the World that lie poking half out of the craggy Ethiopian desert like dead, green teeth. Those villagers could fix anything with an engine, but computer chips were less than useless, they were an insult. So those things sat and were pissed on by the people and the animals there in the Ogaden. Gode, with the beautiful prostitutes that sat and smoked from a hookah all day and fake smiled at whomever was staying in the dirt floored hotel Salim ran at night. Sal was all smiles, but kept a rusty .45 in his belt for "in case." I told Bennett about the little girl with the brain tumor that we tried to get back to the States and about Thomas the war orphan and about the Somali gate guard that killed a viper with a flip flop. I told him about the demon houses and how I marveled at the cooperation between Muslim and Christian when they threw naughty people in those tiny huts in one hundred degree heat. I told him how each of the huts had a corresponding djinn and after sweating them out, the naughty people were either absolved or dead. In the end, it didn't really matter.

I told him that over in those places I felt like a Roman in Judea or a Brit during the Great Game, running west to avenge Elphinstone. I'd been a G.I. in Asia like our fathers. I knew about the dynamism of colonials and about what the powerful do to get it all right for themselves. I told him that it was ugly and devastating but sometimes it was the right thing to do for you and yours. It was a tricky business being ethical in places where people can see children hurt and not flinch. I told him that he knew this was true and that it was the old business and that if people didn't know they'd think we invented this shit in the Philippines in 1900. But we didn't. It was the old magic. Caesar had done it to the Helvetii in Alps. Divide and conquer and bring in the wine and baths and fuck yourselves into a generation that identified with Rome more than some freezing hill fort.

This didn't really happen though. Really, I sat there in his office with the thick books and the brown desk and the cheap rug and didn't say much. I'd tried to interject a few times, but he wanted nothing to do with anything that I had running around in my brain. At the end of the day, that made him fairly obtuse. I'm sure he liked good wine and had a copy of Sketches of Spain somewhere in a pile of records, but that was all handed to him when he put on his uniform. The urban intellectual. I don't think Bennett really thought about other people as humans that bled and coughed and fucked. Or maybe he did. Maybe he had a tumultuous life but refused to believe that anyone else could either. This is also a fault.

So, Bennett stared at me from across his desk. He was bald and tall and had pitchfork hands. He tried very hard to be enigmatic and to speak in psalms. A shit boss for a glacial tomb like Chicago Public Schools, but he'd have been a dynamite entrepreneur. He certainly had a motor.

"I didn't mean they couldn't learn." I said.

"What did you mean?"

"I meant it's frustrating when the kids are disrespectful. Especially when we're trying so hard and getting nowhere."

Bennett exhaled. "See, that's not a good answer. That's when we need to get back in there and really try. You must get back in there and keep working. For them. Keep pressing, and with rigor, and know that you are making a difference." He spoke with his hands and made a motion as though he were screwing in a light bulb when he made a point.

"I agree. I agree." I didn't agree. I didn't really care, not at that time. Not at all. Back then I was as big of a mess as Chicago. I just needed the dough. "I'm not quitting or anything. I wasn't being malicious either. I guess I was just venting. It had been a rough day."

"Well, I hope this clears it up."

"It will, Mr. Bennett. I'm glad we're on the same page."

He stared at me for a while without looking away. It was another silly game he must have learned at a management seminar. A year before, people had been trying to kill me. These tricks meant nothing.

Maybe both of us were alien and trying to fit into this world. Maybe he recognized something of himself in me and he hated what it looked like. Or perhaps I reminded him of someone that had treated him poorly in the past. I don't know. He needed me to be better though. His students were so often the butt of the joke that he guarded tight against threats and mercenary behavior that he saw on the horizon and out the corner of his eye. He railed against that version of ourselves that lurks in the night, grabbing children to drag back into the woods. He saw that in me, even if it wasn't there.

The phone rang and he looked away, motioning to the door like the Pasha of Tripoli. I left and went back to my classroom and the students who were being babysat by a security guard. He rolled his eyes as I walked into the noisy classroom.

"He fuckin with you much?"

"The usual."

"Muthafucka. He's a muthafucka."

HALLOWEEN

SUMMER LASTS THROUGH SEPTEMBER in Chicago. The leaves growing over the side streets in Bucktown show few hints of yellowing until, all of sudden, they're red, and yellow, and brown, and begin to fall into the street. By the end of October, it is still a manageable fifty degrees most of the time, and everyone starts wearing hoodies and coats and pullover hopes that the Bears will win this year. It is pleasant, and the wife and I stay on the porch until we need blankets to sit and listen to the cars rush by.

Halloween comes and the rich turn our neighborhood into a free for all with haunted bungalows and kegs parked on the sidewalk on most blocks. The parents drink beer or wine out of plastic cups and the streets are closed off to cars. The younger children walk with the parents from house to house smiling and pushing candy into their mouths with breath enough only to say "trick or treat" at the next house. The older, newly-minted teens make friends, and mischief their way throughout the blocks to be seen by other twelve and thirteen-year-olds.

The wife and I are no different and drink vodka from plastic cups and steal candy from our son. As he runs from house to house collecting a haul of goodies, we conspire to halve his take by the morning. Our daughter runs with her friends back to Armitage and down to Starbucks. The wife and I wonder if she's kissed a boy yet, or maybe if she tried marijuana. We smile at the families that came from the other side of Western Avenue to get all the good candy and glimpse inside the rich peoples' homes. We felt more akin to them than our neighbors, but really our condo probably costs as much as their houses. Still, we weren't rich. At least not over there. That kind of money doesn't ever think you've been in the running at all, it moves through surf at dusk and is exactly what it is. Successful and vicious and oblivious of you. I think that's what really pisses people off about the rich. It's not that they are malevolent, in person they're usually the opposite, it's that they are not thinking of you at all. Getting mad at them is the single most unrewarding endeavor I can think of. The quarterback didn't pick on you after all, he didn't know you were there.

Our son plays soccer with them, the Mercedes people, the British School Crowd. I admire their honest capacity for clear thought and talent. I've done the ditch digging, and the leaf blowing, and the standing in the sun. It makes you tired and drunk. There's something Christlike about it after all, but at the end of the day, or age forty-five at least, it'd be better to be rich. And twice on Sunday.

THE ESKIMO

LUNT CAME TO US from an artillery unit halfway through the deployment. We were short, and he was sitting around Mehtar Lam doing nothing, so we snatched him up and took him to the outpost. We didn't like the idea that he wasn't an infantryman, but he was young, and we could teach him. And besides, we really were shorthanded.

I stuck him with Corporal Metz to get trained up. After a week of learning the ropes I put Lunt on the fifty cal. on my truck. At first he was scared, but then he leaned into the work and was able to pretend that he wasn't scared, and it gave him purpose. After patrols we clapped Lunt on the back. Metz would joke with him and knock him around in a loving way. They'd get him some smokes and make sure he was at home and one of the guys. It went like this for a while

By January the weather changed, and everything turned scrubby and gray. Lunt stayed in bed unless we were on patrol. He separated himself from the rest of the squad and quit joking around. Then it got much colder and he rarely left his bunk at all. He stopped doing the things a private was supposed to do. I was kind at first. I told him stories of the boys who fought the Sioux out west. I told him he could make it too. I coaxed him and tried to keep him on track. But it didn't work. He hardly spoke. He held heavy things over his head and did lots of pushups and whatever else Metz or I could imagine.

Conversations with Lunt were usually confined to this:

"You've got to be better, Lunt."

Mumble.

"We need you there, on patrol, we're your family over here."

Mumble.

"Did you clean the fifty on the truck?"

Silence.

"See, that's what I'm talking about. Start fucking trying harder, Private."

Again, silence.

"What did you say, Lunt?"

"Yeah."

"Yeah what, Lunt?"

"Yeah, Sarn't."

We knew something was coming. Metz and I spoke about it often. I admit that some part of me actually wanted something to happen to Lunt. Nothing that needed a tourniquet, but something that would shock him back to the squad and the mountain. I went to the platoon sergeant to talk about it.

"There are problems with him," I told him.

"I heard. I don't really care. We need the numbers." We lit cigarettes and drank coffee. Golfer and I were close in age and talked a lot even though he was my boss. "What kind of problems?"

"He's a malingerer or something. Same old thing. He's a fucking shitbag. I think he's too scared to perform."

"Great. We still need him."

"Yeah."

"This is why you get paid all that money, Sarn't."

"Yeah, right."

"It's not like any of us have a choice," he said. "Just make it work."

Our pace didn't slow in January, despite the weather. We went from village to village and then back to the outpost. Day after day we did this. We'd show up, set up security, and talk to the honchos to try and get them on our side. We'd harass Lunt and pull him out of bed. I took him off the fifty and put him on the ground with me where he could do less damage.

Things came to a head at the end of the month. We left early one morning for a village at the end of the valley. Parmawan sat on one side of the river where the road ended. In the spring, the village was bucolic and hidden by trees and the sound of the river. But in the winter, we could see the wooden staircases that sprung from the animal pens to the huts to the walkways. They twisted around the town and were surrounded by open wooden doorways and second and third floor terraces. Little children with black and red hair and in varied states of undress stood and gawked at us from atop stone walls as we walked through their village with weapons and smiles and good teeth.

The lieutenant and his men got to work chatting with the elders. I took my squad up through the town. We peered down alleys. When we raised our rifles, the children scattered. We looked in doors and over walls. We smiled at the kids and the men. We spilled down their alleys like spotted, digital, American water. We moved through the winding, narrow walkways towards high ground above the village. I dropped soldiers along the way. One here, one there. Each man moved within his own little orbit of anger and boredom.

I placed Lunt near the animal pens at the edge of the town. The pens were in a cave covered with branches tied together. These villagers had been doing that for centuries, I'm sure. Lunt stared down into the dark of the cave and waited. I watched him and knew I should have kept him next to me. He stared at the pen and I could see his eyes from where I knelt. They were wide and fixed and he didn't move. He must have thought as we all did, that some angry boy or poor farmer could be hiding behind those branches. Waiting to pull a trigger and send a bullet through his pelvis, or his neck, and he'd lie there bleeding out cold, and alone, there above Parmawan.

The lieutenant and the other squad finished the meeting and called us down. I collected the men. When I passed, they'd nod and silently join in the procession. We made it to Lunt. He sat cross-legged with his back up against a narrow tree. He faced back out at the mountain and the animal pen, oblivious of the meeting, or of Parmawan, or of his friends. Metz picked him up by the arms and got him moving. We had to leave through the village so the gun trucks could cover us. As we walked, the alleys filled with people. The villagers occupied their space again. Shop windows opened. Life came back to Parmawan. Metz was in the rear and turned to walk backwards every few steps. Lunt tried to pass and run to the road in front of me. I put a hand on him and pointed at the trucks. The big guns trained over our heads. "We're fine Lunt."

He looked at me with wide eyes. He didn't see me, or the trucks.

"It's good, man. Chill." Lunt didn't respond. He trudged forward pressing as close to me as he could.

The men of Parmawan watched as we climbed up from the village to the road and the trucks. They no longer smiled. We did this every day. New village, new men. Fear and then anger. And sometimes the anger would get violent. It was exhausting. I put Lunt into his seat and put his rifle between his knees. It fell over onto the floor.

Twelve hours later, there was an attack on the outpost. A Chinese 107 rocket slammed into the supply hut next to the aid station and exploded, shredding toilet paper and ace bandages. There was a silent moment after the explosion and the Afghan machine guns, usually PKMs, started up. Tracers snapped over the tops of barriers and outpost walls.

These night attacks almost always went something like this: The boys threw on their vests. They pulled on their boots, too. They hoot and holler and let fly with lead of their own back out into the night. They run to gun trucks and drive to defensive positions bringing the heavy weapons to bear. Then the mortars ratchet up and everything around the enemy starts to erupt and blow. Either they're killed, or they run out of ammo and split, or a metal bird shows up and sends them scurrying, but no matter what they're eventually gone, and patrols are sent out to look for brass and blood. Those Americans not on the patrol smoke and joke and laugh about the attack, some go right back to sleep, some sit up waiting for more, but the privates, the really young men, tend to be the ones that talk the most shit.

Apparently, Lunt did something to laugh about during the attack and the boys wouldn't let go of it.

By the next evening, things were back to normal. The lieutenants and the sergeants had an intelligence brief and talked about what was heading our way. One of the privates poked his head in the door.

"Sarn't," he was whispering, "Can I talk to you?"

"What is it?"

"Um, you gotta come up to the tents, Sarn't."

I followed him up the hill to the platoon area. The little card table in between the sergeants' tent and the soldiers' tent was overturned and water bottles were spilled into the dirt. There were clothes and boots thrown about in a haphazard way, and an M-16 rifle tossed into the dirt. Two of the soldiers stood over Lunt. They were panting and taunting him. Lunt was hog-tied and on his stomach. His hands were taped behind his back and then taped again, with wide, gray tape to his feet. He snorted and screamed and bucked. One of the soldiers dropped a knee into his back. The other mashed his face down into the plywood walkway. After the knee Lunt didn't say anything.

"Get the fuck off of him!" I said.

"You didn't see what he did Sarn't."

"Yeah, the muthafucka dove behind the Hesco..."

"What?" I said.

"Last night."

"Well they were fucking shooting at us. Get off him."

The chorus of voices continued. "He stayed there, Sarn't. Like a fucking bitch! Stared at our legs the whole time."

"Okay, I get it, untie him."

A knife was out and cutting the tape between his feet and hands. Metz and I grabbed Lunt by the shoulders and started to haul him up as Sergeant Golfer rounded the corner.

"What the fuck?" he whispered.

The boys broke into the story about Lunt diving behind cover and staying there for the whole attack.

There was a pause and the kid he had started fighting with said, "He pointed his fucking weapon at me."

Golfer looked at me. I shrugged, staring at the boys.

"What?" said Golfer.

"After dinner chow we were sitting around joking and teasing him.

He pointed that fucking M16 at me and said he'd kill me if I didn't stop calling him a bitch. Then he racked a round and that's when I fucked him up."

The boys all nodded.

Sergeant Golfer asked, "Lunt. Is this true?"

Metz and I were still holding him.

"Is it true Lunt? I asked him. "What happened?"

He said nothing. He just looked at the ground.

The next morning Lunt was in the supply shack next to the outhouses. The shack was wooden and built like an outhouse but had been full of toilet paper and hand sanitizer. Now it was where Lunt sat staring at the inside of its wooden door for days on end. He ate twice a day and had a stash of water in there with him. Every couple of hours Sergeant Golfer would check on him and get a barely audible, "yeah."

By the end of the week a helicopter came to pick him up and he was gone. That was it.

Occasionally squads would head down to Mehtar Lam to refit and upon returning would say that they saw him at the chow hall, or in the room with the computers, beanie cocked down over one eye, moving around like nothing had happened.

I didn't see him again until July when all the units from the battalion linked back up at Bagram to prepare for the trip home. The reunited platoons and companies joked around and packed and got everything in order and accounted for and ready to go. The serial numbers were checked. The weapons were cleaned. Our clothes were washed, and we drank decent coffee for the first time in months. We wore clean clothes and shit in air-conditioned bathrooms. We were safe. During all this movement, a pair of night vision goggles went missing. The serial numbers said they belonged to the platoon. Golfer and I and Corporal Metz spent the waking hours of a very hot day searching through every item of baggage, first in the company, and then the battalion area. Spilling rucksacks. Upending green and black Tac boxes. Rifling through used and tattered uniforms. It wasn't till a few hours past dark that the goggles were found. They were, somehow unsurprisingly, found at the bottom of Private Lunt's rucksack.

It's easy to see now, with civilian's eyes, that we could wind up the vile ones in this story. The Wolves of Najil Town, or something. I told this story to some friends at a party once and they were silent and stared at their hands. But it made sense when it happened, even if it left me with a feeling that something was wrong. You don't go to war with choirboys after all, or nice boys, or boys that do what they're told. The ones that get put on the mountain start to run when the leash comes off. The military doesn't make them that way; it takes those that have a penchant for that line of work, and they give it four walls and a roof. They give it prayer.

If this were a movie about anti-heroes, then Lunt could have been a redeeming character. He could have been childlike and beatific. He could have been unbending. But it wasn't a movie. He didn't understand the rules there on the mountain. Hawkeye, and Trapper, and Yossarian would have been shit-canned or had their noses flattened if they'd been on an outpost in the mountains. It was that way for Lunt.

DISRAELI GEARS

THERE WERE SIGNS OF THE BRITISH WARS in that part of
the country. They were half buried, of course, but they were there and
fused with the mud and the rearing of children. Maybe the Afghans
on television had changed, the rich ones that schooled at Oxford and
Cambridge. But there, in the mountains in the east, not much had
changed in one hundred and forty years. There were still the sabers and
the donkeys and rocks and wicker baskets. There were the goats and the
shit and the painted boys that got passed around by men in the village.
And then we arrived and added annoyance, and sometimes horror and
death. But we would leave, and whatever we had brought and built
would bury over with sand and bones a year after we were gone.

I have memories of a moment when I became separated from
the main. It was only for a few minutes, and there are memories of
worse things that I keep buried most of the time. But this one comes

whenever it wants. Just for a second, electric jolts while I'm driving, or in a moment to myself, and then I shiver and exhale and forget the feeling for a couple more days.

It was in the pitch black hours between midnight and sun up. We walked for a few hours. We crossed the Mayl River, climbed up and over the plateau, up and through the craggy foothills of the mountain. We'd started around midnight, and a few hours later we finally crested the last and highest hill on our route. Once over it the valley opened beneath us and we could see a light here or there, a twinkling hearth, marking the villages that dotted the ridgeline. They were stepping stones that led to the Dowlat Shah and beyond, to the truly lawless place. We weren't going there yet though, that morning it was for the first village after the crest. It was for Bumby.

We'd split into two groups, looking for the passage down the mountain to reach positions over the town by dawn. My group swung like a gate down and across a section of the hillside, through the sparse trees, and over the rocks that rolled with booted feet. I was trying to be quiet and slick, but then, separation. I turned back and there wasn't anyone there. It was too dark on this side of the mountain for my night vision to work that well. Every shadow became the enemy, and they knew I was there, they smelled me, they could see in the dark like cats that padded from tree to tree waiting to grab me and drag me down to be lost forever, pin cushioned like the British stragglers racing for Jalalabad more than a century before.

A few months before this, before the night patrol to Bumby, we heard a bad man named Fazil Rabi was near our outpost in a place called Kanday. We surrounded the village while the Afghan National Army, along with our lieutenants, searched the buildings. We'd missed Mr. Rabi—"the Lion," the people called him—he'd slipped out as we got into position, but the search of the village paid off. There are pictures of the smiling lieutenants with stacks of rocket launchers and light machine guns, hundreds of rounds in boxes strewn about, a Russian automatic grenade launcher most of us had never seen before and there, in the center of it all, a Martini-Henry rifle. The imperial rifle. The British pilum. Rusted and wood-scuffed, the century-plus-old-action still worked, ready to fire the ugly, blunt-nosed rifle rounds they were used to firing back in the days of Victoria and Disraeli.

How is it possible, I thought later, that it had all led to me, alone on the way to Bumby, separated and in the trees, trying not to breathe and shrinking around my rifle? All of the time and calamity that traversed these mountains: the Persians, the Macedonians, and the Sassanids; the Hephthlalites, the Khwarazmians, the Mongols, the Mughals, and the Brits and their damned Martini-Henrys. Then the Russians and the slaughter; there was a tiny graveyard on our outpost, next to the LZ, the product of a Soviet purge. All of it, all of time in those mountains ground out, stopping and starting again throughout the ages had unraveled to me, and I was at its breakwater, I was the prow, alone.

Kneeling in the dark as all of this welled up inside me, I put my rifle to my cheek and began turning from side to side, listening, scanning with the safety off. Searching. It's all time travel anyway. I could have been there on the shale leaning against that thin tree for an hour— maybe a millennia—but it hadn't been. It was only after a few moments that I saw an infrared signal. There was a flash in the dark, then two flashes, I sent back three, and that was it. The other section had found the passage in the direction they'd been sent. I walked back up the hill and linked up with the squad, the squad that I was then supposed to lead through the night to the town of Bumby to surprise some man or another.

I know he was there, though. Maybe he was scared of me as well. Maybe I was so close I could have dashed his brains out with my rifle. As it was, I'm glad I didn't piss myself. We were all brave when next to one another; even with only one other, we could be brave. As long as someone would be able to bolster you with love, or shame, or brotherhood, or whatever, then you could be brave. But alone is a different story. There were nights at the outpost that I could swear he was crawling up on us. I knew it, crawling up and cutting the wires while we huddled, freezing in guard shacks, all together, periodically staring at the mountains. Crawling up the stairs to the outpost while we dozed at the guns, fighting off sleep till morning. The tide would always come in.

CANTON

MY GRANDFATHER CAME HOME from France in 1945. He had fought along the Rhine at Remagen. He'd been captured drunk in a barn, shot through the face, and then escaped. He made it back to Ohio after the war and started working on the Boom. I'm not sure how long it took him to get the job, but he started laying bricks at the furnace in downtown Sugar Creek. His name was Ulysses, and that's true. Ulysses was a sweet man who would bounce my sister and I on his knee. At some point he took on Jesus and would only drink on the holidays. I remember him wearing those terry cloth shirts that had a cigarette pocket over the heart. He smoked Winstons and when he wore short sleeves, I could see the tattoos he'd picked up overseas. They had taken on a bluish green tint by that time. He seemed old but was probably fifty-five.

I remember tracing the panther on his right forearm. My sister and I focused on that one and only stole sideways glances at the nude woman draped around a dagger on his other arm. Ulysses was friends with the other blue-collar men in town. Really, there were only blue-collar men in Sugar Creek back then, but there were also the Amish. They rode buggies on 77 and waved to Ulysses when we'd drive by in his Oldsmobile. He was my Mom's dad and she said he was the sweetest man she ever knew. My Grandmother used to make Waldorf Salad in big plastic bowls on Thanksgiving while we watched football. Once I hit about twelve Ulysses would make jokes about the Dallas Cowboy cheerleaders. He'd look around for my Grandmother and my parents and then make gestures with his hands that I didn't really understand for another year. Ulysses died my Freshman year at Dayton. My mom called me crying and told me that he'd died at dinner while out with his kids and his wife. I think the Winstons got to him in the end, but I bet if you asked that boy hiding in a cellar by the Rhine the kind of life he needed to lead to buy himself forty-five more years, he'd say that's just fine.

THESE ARE JUST THE NORMAL NOISES

AND THIS IS HOW IT WENT. Up one side, through the village, and then back down again. Set up, take down, wake the drowsy men. Squint into the mountains for movement, radio checks, get a grid, VS17 panels, a quick barber brush to your weapon, squeeze of peanut butter, water, water, cigarettes, check your magazine, check on the Afghans, some more water, pissing from a knee at a security halt and over and over again. Then back to base, clear your weapons, after action review, fuel the trucks, fix the trucks, cover the guns, smoke and joke, watch a movie and wait for chow, wait for the best outhouse, shower every ten days. Meetings for the sergeants and the lieutenant: planning, manning, more grids, routes, water and holy smokes; dinner chow, Halo, talking shit, more Halo, talk to Sarn't about tomorrow, clean your weapons, smoke, get chow and equipment for the morning, should get rest but more Halo and shit-talking until your guard shift, finish, pass out, and get woken up by Corporal Metz. And so it went: monotonous, exciting, exhausting dreams in a mountain paradise fighting bronze age warriors armed with Russian gear that thought you were the devil.

The shura ended and it was on to the third village. We packed up and moved down, through the town, past our friends, nodded to the LT, and moved across the road. We passed the trucks and the willow tree and the women farming with hoes. Their children played amongst the farming tiers that led down from the road into the valley floor. The kids always asked for our pens and pencils. Once we passed, they shot slingshots at birds and each other and us.

The women spoke with one another as they farmed and seemed to ignore the twenty armed Americans as we wound through the tall grass, over the tiny stone walls, along the irrigation ditches, and over ground we could not see until it broke to the open riverbed, and stone, and the bridge. The bridge was only a plank of wood over the river, balanced on piles of rocks and a muddy bank. The water rushed beneath us as we crossed. Mostly no one spoke, only sweated, and swore, and stared, blinking through the sweat to see all around them. Sergeants counted their men from one side of the river to the other, placing them safely on the other side. The men behind them would then cross and push through them and take the lead up the next hill, to the next town. It was a smooth and practiced movement, the men passing one another and fanning out when terrain would allow. Sometimes a sergeant would whistle at a soldier and point and the man would correct his movement and the dance continued like water being poured from one shape to another until it halted and then disappeared, sinking into the terrain in front of the next town.

Metz and I set the men in and moved amongst them keeping them awake and watchful. When they were ready, I would look at the lieutenant and he'd nod or say "roger" into the radio and we'd wait for the word to move in through the town. Everything was fluid and the men wouldn't remember much of what they did that day, but they were aware of that moment and how it was much cooler at the river than here, in the dirt. They would remember how the grass smelled and how it mixed with the shit from the animal pens.

At home they'd gotten speeches by their officers about how they were sheepdogs. They were told that their job was to keep the wolf away from the door. But in Afghanistan they were reptiles. They were still and moved only when they had to. They dozed on rocks and measured the world. They lapped at the air with tongues and hid under bushes and pretended to be asleep.

The LT gave the nod and we raised the men up with our hands. We were in control of the earth. We moved the men up through a stone ditch. The sharp rocks and overhanging trees must have been a beautiful, painful nuisance the last time the British were there, with Kipling and the Great Game. Water trickled down through the slough as we moved up through it and fanned out around the town.

The LT and half the men stayed in the town for the meeting with the elders. Metz and I took our men through the town and up, above the village to a hut overlooking the meeting. We cleared the hut and set up shop all over again. Wilson scanned the crowd of locals around the shura for weapons. He watched our Lieutenant and his retainers talk with sixty-year-old Afghans. He saw kohl-lined eyes and dyed-red beards listen to our truths and pleas for compliance. He watched our soldiers pass out human assistance packages while the Afghans served tea.

From above the village Metz and I looked over the surrounding area, marking the routes from which the enemy could best approach and pointed men and weapons at those places. I pulled out the map and we again plotted out those points with a protractor, measuring the angles and distances from us to what bothered us and writing it all down on paper. We checked the radios, flashed our panels, and told the trucks where we were. We prepped our fire missions with the mortars in case someone tried to intervene with the Great-Bean-Giveaway that was happening down below in the village. It was rehearsal after rehearsal and done with the least amount of consciousness. These drills came from somewhere in our spines. It was the third one that day.

Metz and I didn't think much of home at times like this. We were working and repeating things to one another. But the men, lying amongst the rocks with rifles pointed at nothing but stone and wood flickered in and out of reality. When one turned off the others turned on and we sat there in the center, he and I, watching them, waking them, pulling them from the molasses sleep of the exhausted. We pulled them from thoughts of Chicago and the L and the weekend festivals that they were missing. A soldier remembered the way a girl had spoken to him and how she seemed cool and like the river that glided through the valley below him. We pulled them from this and back to the mountain, to a path or a rocky outcrop at which to point a gun.

The shura ended, the aid passed out, pictures taken, and we prepared to go; folding the laminated map back into my pocket and checking weapons and equipment to make sure we left nothing, not even a peanut butter packet, for the assholes that were sure to come and see where we were now laying. They would come and see what we were seeing and try to figure out how to get around us next time. We picked up everything and moved back down through the town to the shura and passed through everyone and kept walking back down, through the slough. We were the water, pouring again from a basin to a jar and then back again.

We crossed the plank bridge and spread out on the other side of the river, folding into stonewalls and boulders and looking back into the town and the hillside as our friends pushed across the plank. They moved silently through us, a noise here or there as a rifle barrel clanged against a rock or a boot crunched something underfoot. We moved past the riverbed, through the tall grass that covered the ground, and over the ditches and small stonewalls.

It took us a long time to cross the valley floor. The men were tired and not as fast as they had been that morning. They knew we were heading back to base and under the eyes of the trucks and their heavy weapons. They glided from obstacle to obstacle, slithering on their rear ends over the three-foot stonewalls that separated the farm plots in the valley floor. Heads down along little berms that shored the irrigation ditches; if one man stopped suddenly, he would run into the man in front of him. They sweated, and their helmet's straps cut into their chins and their cheeks. They reached the women farmers and their kids. The women spoke with each other as they worked the hoes. The kids still played and ran around their mothers. The trucks and their weapons watched the ridgeline over our heads as we climbed our way out of the valley to the willow tree and the road in front of Uluk. The men reached the road and laughed with their friends on the trucks. We drank water and lit cigarettes. The men climbed into the trucks and we got radio checks with all the vehicles. The lieutenant called the outpost and told them we were coming home. We sank into the uncomfortable, green seats.

I would've done it while we were stumbling through the riverbed, but for some reason they waited until we made it back to the trucks before trying to kill us. Maybe they came from the town itself and had to climb up to the top of the ridgeline. Maybe they were tired too. Maybe they didn't really want a blood war but had started a fight just to show off for the people that would murder their families if they hadn't.

For whatever reason, they waited, and I had no idea they were there until a rocket slammed into the terrace to the right of my truck. It exploded with a loud, two-syllable sound. Only a puff of white smoke was visible. The grass was a deep green and the cloud looked like cotton. If you are aware of the launch, then there's a second or two when every breath eats itself and every muscle in your body is clenched, assholes puckered, as they say. And then the rocket explodes and you're either safe or you're not. This time it was only the cracking of the air and then the ghost. I stared at it out of my window.

Another rocket slammed into the terrace near us. Machine gun fire landed in the grass just below our trucks, too. The radio had come to life with the first rocket. Everyone spoke at once. Our machine guns started firing. The enemy was firing at us but was coming short, plunging their fire into the women and children farmers. I watched one of the Afghan women, her robes were purple and yellow and red, dash through the tall plants and gunfire to grab her children and hide behind a low stonewall that marked the end of her property, ten feet away from where I sat in the truck. All of this played just outside of my window.

Her face was drawn, and I could see her teeth. The muscles in her cheeks were tensed and she had her arms around her boys. She clutched them to her breast and tried to cover them with her tilted head. She looked at me. She looked specifically at my face through the thick glass. Her eyes were black, I think, I couldn't see the color really, but they stretched from her place, wedged in between the ground and the stone wall and her children to me in the truck. We were linked. The armored trucks fired over their heads and sent brass and links clanging down onto the top of the trucks and into the grass. She stared at me with those eyes and her drawn lips. They distilled helplessness and parenthood and the fear of losing everything in seconds to me as I sat there dumb, and in sunglasses, and armor.

Sam was our skinny nineteen-year-old gunner. He was afraid of heights so when we were walking on higher ground we kept him with the trucks on the gun. He started firing the fifty on the top of the truck as soon as it all began. He was shooting across the valley floor to the ridgeline, four hundred meters away. The sound of the fifty was comforting and masculine and hammered away from above and behind my seat. He raked the ground with the large, armor-piercing, rounds. They were incendiary and terrifying, and sparks flashed every time one of them drove into a rock or a tree. Fear and anger hurtled across the valley from the road to the ridgeline and back again. Sam kept firing until he burned through a can of ammunition.

The lieutenant's truck was in the lead and started pulling forward. We had six trucks on the patrol and I was in the rear. The other four trucks, the ones in between the LT and my vehicle stayed in place.

I keyed the mic, "Move forward!" I tried to stay calm on the radio, but it came out like a shout.

Another rocket landed somewhere I couldn't see. The smoke from the first two rockets hovered over where they'd landed. Two more clouds the size of men.

We started to move when the rear passenger door swung open. The doors are armored and heavy and hard to manage. It swung open towards the ridgeline and the shooting and then bounced back. Al, who was sitting in that seat, grabbed the handle and slammed it shut but it bounced open again. The trucks were weathered and battered, and the door needed to be tied shut with cord to stay in place. Al didn't like the idea of being trapped in case we got in a fight, so he had cut it and had held it shut during the patrol. Now it flapped open and shut like a kid's cape getting blown about as he ran down the road.

Sam was yelling down through the turret hatch. "Ammo!" The interpreter in the back behind the driver was fumbling with the straps holding the ammo cans.

A higher pitched firing, very rapid, blasted out from behind my seat. I didn't know where it came from, but I knew it had to be the enemy in the Uluk, firing down from the village behind us.

We would laugh about this later in the tents. It was Sam, again.

He kept an automatic rifle in the turret with him and when the fifty ran out of ammunition he had grabbed his other weapon almost immediately, spraying the smaller, lighter rounds across the valley into the ridgeline. I could see puffs of smoke from all our trucks' weapons arising all along the ridgeline as bullets slammed into the side of the mountain. It looked like a child throwing handfuls of sand into a pond, over and over and over, hitting everything. If the enemy was still there, he was dead. It was more likely he'd crested the ridgeline and lie, hidden behind a rock formation with his partners, smoking and praying before starting to shoot again.

Al fumbled with the door, grabbing the cut parachute cord with both hands: "Fucking door!"

The automatic rifle stopped firing and Sam's hands reached down through the turret.

"Come on!"

The interpreter freed a can of ammo.

"I've got it. Here. Here. Fucking bullets!"

He passed the ammo to Sam who began reloading the fifty. We started moving forward. Metz was driving and could only see the truck in front of him. He leaned forward, staring through the windshield, both hands on the steering wheel. The guns kept firing. The men were awake. I was aware of everything. My entire body was there, sitting in the front seat of the truck. The only thing one can do from the front of a Humvee is talk on the radio and look out the window or at the computer map screen next to you. It's a tight fit. It's difficult to even slide the tiny, thick window open. I sat, staring at the ridgeline and at the trucks in front of us, cheering as Sam fired into the mountain. We all cheered and cursed and yelled. Metz smacked Sam's legs with his right hand, egging him on as he hammered away with the big machine gun.

The radio was silent except for the LT. "Push. Push. Push."

It must have only been a minute since the fight began and now the column was moving forward, still firing into the ridgeline. Everyone was awake and aware of his body again. Al realized the parachute cord was cutting off the circulation to his hand as he pulled on the door. All I could do from my seat was monitor the radio and look through my window at the ridgeline getting beaten by thousands of tiny bullets.

Our truck passed out of the ambush and we were no longer in the thick of it. Sam stopped firing as we rolled. We passed the rock wall where the women and their children were hiding, shrunken but alive, and one with the place where the stone touched the earth, pouring themselves into the base of the thing becoming as small as the rest of the human life that battled the mountain for existence. The interpreter asked for a cigarette. There was a pack behind the computer screen. I passed some to Metz and the interpreter and lit one, handing it up though the turret to Sam.

And that's how it ended. A flurry of violence and awareness. The fights always erased the patrols, or the three AM guard shifts at the OP, or whatever else you'd been doing that day. An exchange of steel, and emotion, and "just wanting to kill those motherfuckers" that lasted for two minutes, or two days. It was time travel and separate from the laudanum of a hot spring day or a midnight barrage. It was a flurry and then there was nothing but the mountain and the river and reptiles. After a fight it was always like that, there was always a return to the quiet, eternal sounds. The men were tired but now they were exhilarated, and still alive, and by the time we returned to base were bickering about pulling guard that night and teasing one another.

CLEVELAND

EVERY FRIDAY AT SIX, Kid Leo would play Born to Run. Every Friday, Born to Run and then Friday on My Mind. It was comforting, and those big chords and Springsteen's warble clanging out of the radio told us it was the weekend. Cleveland really fit the Springsteen ethos and, aside from football, the freedom dream sold by the Boss was all we needed. The wistful dreamer stories draped us in a place that allowed us to all become underdogs. We were punchy and rambunctious. We were outside dogs. We made out with girls just as punchy in the Metroparks. None of us put on airs, they would have been sniffed out and eradicated. It was always us against them. Us versus the rest of you. Even the middle class somehow felt under the gun by the rest of the country. There's something comforting in knowing you'll be underestimated. One gets used to it and punches that much harder, screams that much louder, and when it doesn't work, offers a beatific fuck you to the victor.

"We never expected to beat you, you cunt, we just wanted to hurt you!"

Even Detroit, with its toughness and the downtrodden masses still thinking of themselves as cool because, you know, Motown comes from there. And the fucking Stooges, man. But not Cleveland. Some of the Dads beat the boys, and some did not. Some of the boys had cars on blocks in the front yard, others were tied to the mob, still others the suburban bliss. But in the end, we were more like one another than an outsider. You want to head to one of those places and start some trouble? Good luck.

SOLON

THE STUDENTS COULDN'T LISTEN. Their little hormone engines hummed along and clanged so loudly they couldn't hear what he was trying to say. This understanding of their station in life didn't help the teacher with compassion. He hated them. He pretended to like them, but he hated them for reminding the teacher at every turn that he was a teacher. The common, and patronizing, take on this career path was that it was noble, and that it was difficult. But he knew better and had worked with his back, and had fought, and had experienced what real work was and knew all that "teachers fight the good fight" stuff was bunk. It was masturbation. The hard part was continuing to stand there in front of his students, screaming into the ether.

He began having waking fantasies of burning the building down. He realized that sounded kooky, or perhaps like he shouldn't be teaching at all, but there it was, he wanted to burn that fucking building down.

The last time he taught he had the same reaction. Actually, it had been worse, with vomiting in the mornings. Puking in the trash can and then hiding it in the bathroom just before the students got there. The last time, a national tragedy had come along and he'd joined the army and gotten away from it. He had ideas about doing something new after getting out, but as his life's goals all rested with the artistic—and that is to say, goals that rarely paid a dime—he went back to teaching after doing seven years on the gun.

So, there he was. Wind up the top and keep it spinning as the steam escapes. Put walls around it and you're dead.

This is how the days went for a long time. Years even. He'd been home from the war for seven years now and almost everyone he knew was tired of hearing about it. He stared at forty-five and another year in the classroom and knew that some transmogrification had to take place, or this would be it. A slow, stale crawl towards a death hastened by alcoholism, immobility, and strife.

He tried talking with his coworkers often.

"You know, I heard she was sleeping with him when he was still a student here."

"Sleeping with him?"

"Yes."

"In her classroom?"

She laughed. "I guess. It's gross."

The kid was seventeen and Ms. Duncan was twenty-two.

"Well, the kid wasn't ten or anything."

"Still. It's fucked up though, isn't it?" She wasn't really asking.

"Yeah, it's worse that she crossed the line."

"Right."

"Twenty-two year olds have zero mileage. I'm sure she didn't understand the dynamic. Or maybe she just didn't care. Maybe she was enlightened."

"Yeah, well she's gone now."

The teachers kind of chuckled to one another.

"Jesus Christ, if I'd done it, I would be in jail."

"No kidding."

The job was punctuated by these little office flair ups. Many of the teachers had only been teachers, professionally speaking, and had been doing it since they were in their twenties. They'd left high school for Bowling Green or Purdue and four years later had gone right back to high school and began to mimic what they saw every day. They fit back into the hallways and arguments they'd left just four or five years before. Hierarchies and ideas of what's attractive, or desirable, or noble, were hung on them like a cape that changed slightly from year to year. They moved with the wind as new crops of teenagers came and went. Sometimes it's hard to grow up if you can't see what's really going on.

A year or so after he'd gotten back from the war he waited for ten minutes to use the copier because two middle-aged teachers were fighting the same fight they'd had for ten years in front of it, over paper, or over order of preference, or just because they hated their lives and were striking out like drowning people for a rope thrown from shore. At first, he thought it was funny. Then he saw that this was it. This is what life is to become, he told himself. A world utterly without chaos, a world so rigid, and so preplanned, that the hours of the day were punctuated by an actual bell telling him when he could move. Confrontations were over copy paper and shared fridge space. And it began to eat away at him.

"I need you to run for union steward," the principal said.

"What? Mr. Bennett, why?" The teacher didn't care about the union at all.

"Well, really it's like a union liaison. Between the rep and the rest of the staff. You seem to get along with most of the people and I'd like to know what the hell's going on."

"You want me to be the Tribune of the Plebs!" He got excited.

The principal stared at him.

"The Tribune of the Plebs. You know, like Marc Antony when the senate tried to rough him up. The Gracchi Brothers. Sticking up for the little guy and all."

The principal did not move. He only looked at him. "I'd like it if you went and put your name in today."

"Okay." And on it went.

He went to meetings to listen to the complaints from worker bees about incidents that should be brought up with administration. The biggest take away was that Mrs. So-and-So really hated it when Mr. So-and-So, the Dean of Students, sent "bossy" emails that didn't contain a salutation. Later, the problems became real, and hard to solve, with questions about pay and pension and quality of life. But Chicago was gutted, and Illinois was broke. They all should have run.

The students often interacted with each other sexually. It was appropriate for their age, but it made him uncomfortable. He remembered being like that as a kid and shuddered. They'd poke and prod one another, clumsily touching breasts with out of place stretches, or leans from one desk to another. In Afghanistan he'd watched a guy fuck a dog through an infrared scope. He had trouble believing it, the dog-fucking, but once Danny called him up to the look-out platform, above the sandbagged hut with the Mark 19, they sat laughing awkwardly and taking turns watching the scene through the device. The teacher wasn't ready to compare any of his students to dogs, they were just adolescents after all, but the feeling was the same. He was watching something so clumsy, and so honest. He was watching something so human that acknowledging it would be embarrassing. He was a voyeur and a passenger who sat behind his desk at the back of the room.

At some point in late fall the head coach of the football team was shouldered out. He was bad at his job and boasted seasons that usually amounted to two or three haphazard wins. When the new coach came, and the teacher met him and liked him, he decided to help out and start coaching. The teacher had come up in Ohio, with the football religion, and had played and done well. Now, working with the young players, away from their girlfriends and away from their classrooms, he got to know them as young men. He felt at home with the players and could push them physically, and train them to do the right thing. They were honest in everything on the field. Off the field they played and pawed at each other in a way that made the coaches feel like they were doing something worth a damn.

He tried to instill the fundamentals and a sense of toughness. The teacher knew that if they could tackle that much better, and block more aggressively, and play to the whistle, they could beat the other city teams their size.

These boys were as rattled as his soldiers overseas. They were only a year or two younger than infantry privates and had lived with a threat of violence their whole lives. It could spike at any time and one's neighbor could have his brains blown out on the sidewalk with no warning. When it wasn't kinetic it would simmer, and it would hum, low and in the background and this hum kept everyone in a state of flinching and scanning the crowd for danger. This lasted from April to January in a real way, and then died down because of the bitter cold in the winter. The winter, too cold to do anything outside for very long, was the safest season of the year.

At any rate, the teacher had his favorites. Darnell was smart. His girlfriend was smart too. When the teacher talked to him about using condoms the cornerback said, "Come on, Coach. Of course! We're going to college." As a junior, Darnell asked the teacher if he could switch into his Advanced Placement class. He did and loved writing papers and reading essays by Aristotle and Cicero.

At the end of his junior year Darnell came to the coaches and told them he couldn't play his senior year. His Dad was dying. Darnell was going to miss all of summer practice and at least the first few games. He needed a job to help his mom pay for things. He needed to become a man, for real, and earlier than was expected. He said all of this with a resolution and an acceptance that this was simply the way things had to be.

Getting from his parents' house in the Austin neighborhood to work in Lincoln Park was fraught with the kind of dangers and pitfalls that the Greeks adored. The least of which was a long bus ride. It went through several neighborhoods, each one patrolled by different and competing groups of young men with very little hope. Darnell was safe walking from his block to the corner, but then it was often a foot race to Cicero and Madison where he'd get the bus north to Armitage and then that bus east before it hit Kedzie and the white boys who didn't shoot. Sometimes he took the blue line by the highway, but had to head all the way to the loop before he could switch and head up the shoreline to Lincoln Park. He liked the bus more. This was his seventeen-year-old life.

Darnell didn't show throughout August two-a-days. He wasn't there to mentor the pudgy underclassman, or to sweat with his peers, to deal with the headaches and sore body that come from those long, glorious days. Before the third game of the year, Darnell came to the coaches and asked to get back on the team. The coaches said of course, and he hugged them for it. He started that next game. By

October he was excellent.

The weekend before the homecoming game saw twenty-three shootings. It was considered a manageable number. Two days before the game the team's best lineman got assaulted by a woman with a bowie knife at the bus stop. He broke her jaw and then set her unconscious body gingerly on the bus stop bench and called 911. They were good boys.

After the homecoming game Darnell was on his way home when a couple of kids who he knew from the neighborhood tried to rob him at the bus stop. When he told them to fuck off one of the boys pulled a knife and slashed his forearm. The blade cut through his shirt and through the tendon and he couldn't lift his hand any longer. He'd gotten to play four or five games. He'd played well, too. A couple interceptions and good tackles and really just being there emanating confidence and modeling what the others were supposed to do did wonders for the team. It was important. But then it was over. He spent the next couple months in bandages. The doctors reattached the tendon and he regained use of his hand, but it left a big scar that showed when he cuffed his shirts bagging groceries at the Mariano's in Lincoln Park.

It was enough to make the teacher sick. The little ball of unease that rolled around in his chest heated up. Put walls around it and you're dead. But the teacher knew about obligation, he'd worked with his back and he'd fought. He needed his kids, his own children, to have insurance, and the fine things his students didn't have.

He realized that what most people called "real life" was only a narrow passageway. They were horses in stable stalls, tricked into thinking that the stalls were the prairies out west. They'd been convinced that this is how they wanted it to be, that this life is the best life. But it was a lie, and a construct, and he realized that they were too big for the stable. They were too tall and couldn't look up or down without falling over. They were standing on a pin. They couldn't really even turn around. A little to the left or a little to the right. That was it. Those were the choices. Just continue to stand there and eat and shit and wait to keel over in a couple years. It's what kept him from buying into the job, or other people for that matter. He waited and planned to get his kids out and move them somewhere without the hordes of people shuffling through intersections staring at their phones oblivious of the traffic and death speeding by them.

The boys won most of their games. Most of the teams they played could barely snap the ball. But it still meant something to them. And therefore, it meant something to the teacher. During the season, the little things stopped bothering him so much. Arguments over copiers became nothing. Arguments over political opinions no longer bothered him either. Any deviation invited wrath and ostracism anyway. He simply didn't care now and thought only about how to help these young men become realized, and hopeful, and to win at something that brought them confidence. In their regular lives they were almost always told to dial back any version of masculinity that came naturally. They were told that who-they-are, on the inside, is obvious, and aggressive, and that what they feel naturally is passé and brutish. At least on the field these boys were giving everything for a chance to win out in some measure. Many of the boys didn't have much else.

And then he went home for a reunion. And he saw the kids play in Northeast Ohio. The suburban kids in stadiums and new gear and painted faces. He'd played there in high school and whenever he tried to explain what it was like, the size of it, his players didn't get it. And he knew that the team he was coaching was bad, and that it wasn't their fault. They were in a system that prevented them from being slightly more than terrible. And if it were a movie maybe an emotional director would have the poor kids win. But in reality, if they played one another his boys would probably get hurt. They might get a first down, might. Those boys with the sixty-five man teams and the weight rooms and ten years of preparation and, most importantly, the belief that they were going to win and that losing was a fucking sin, would beat those city boys by sixty or seventy points. Really, they'd beat them by as many points as the clock would allow. He didn't blame the suburban boys, they didn't hate the city boys, they just knew they'd beat them to death and wanted to, because they wanted to beat everyone down. That's what they were trained to do, and bred to do, and would do. It wasn't malice so much as inertia. They'd smile uncynically and help our boys up after cracking their ribs.

So, the teacher quit coaching and went back to the classroom. He no longer wanted to lie to his players, it weighed too much. He rejoined the conversations in the copy room and attended the union meetings.

He went back to the stable stall and shut the barn door himself. He'd worked with his back, and fought, and knew the smoke getting blown up the teachers' asses was all bunk. But it paid, and it got insurance for his kids, so he doubled down and got the mortgage and the car note and worried about election cycles as though any of that mattered at all.

QAL'EH NAJIL

THIS WAS THE BUSINESS of swimming with sharks. It was the business of waiting, and walking, and guessing if they'd hit you in the front or the rear. Whole conversations were dedicated to the finer points of luck on a patrol. It really was location and timing. The violence would come with the hills, screaming down and the road bursting, pushing us hundreds of feet down, into a river. The fear of burning to death as bullets cooked off behind your head or lying broken, drowning in two feet of river, made us eager for the long foot patrols we took in the mountains. It was the IEDs that scared us. It was the unknown death, reaching through the earth from beneath our feet, hurtling through armor and taking everything away. These conversations consumed whole guard shifts and packs of cigarettes.

We laughed about these things from our bunks, but not when we climbed into the trucks for another patrol, holding our breath and riding with our feet light on the floor like kids past a cemetery.

THE GADFLY

EUGENE WASN'T THE BEST LOOKING eighteen-year-old in Warrick County. In school pictures his features were too ruddy and too outsized. And his hair was more like a pelt than anything a coed would ever want to run her fingers through. I'm sure his mother felt differently though, and honestly, when he was in motion, he was beautiful. Many of the young soldiers were like Eugene. They were nineteen or twenty and had left their parents' care for the Army's. They were probably more rambunctious than their peers at Madison or Palo Alto, but after six months in the army they are more competent than a frat boy, and for the most part act with the knowledge that they have more to prove to the world. There's a hubris that comes from knowing that they're the ones that will take it in the face when everything goes all to hell. We like them that way, too.

He'd come to us straight out of basic training. And that had come directly after a lackluster four years in high school. He was light, and tough, and easily wore the smallest uniform in the platoon. Sometimes he'd ask out of the blue, "Sarn't, permission to smoke myself?" Then he'd jump to the ground and bang out fifty push-ups or mountain climbers and pop up laughing at the big joke and at being so hooah. His buddies were also super gung-ho and had a sense of humor about it too. They started copying him with the whole push-up thing when they felt like it. When he insisted on being on a gun team, his friends did too. When we asked him why, he smiled and said, "I wanna make that Pig my bitch, Sarn't." The Pig is a light machine gun common to an infantry platoon. It's a sleek, devastating weapon that the fittest, or biggest, privates get selected to carry. "Light" is relative only to the "heavy" machine guns that were usually attached to vehicles or guard towers. It's about as tall as Eugene, and probably a third as heavy. Just carrying the ammo was a separate job, but he wanted to have the roughest, deadliest, weapon in the squad.

Eugene would ask questions whenever there was silence, maybe while we were running in the morning, or cleaning weapons, or during some other monotonous task that prompted the boys to start shit talking. "Sarn't, will a twenty-five-millimeter round make a body explode?" or, "Hey Jason, you think there'd be anything worse than getting buried alive?" His eyes were blue and kind of sparkled at the person as he spoke to them in a southern Indiana drawl. Often, he knew the answers to his questions and was already smiling when he asked them. Sometimes they were directed at his comrades. "Damien, you think you'll marry that stripper girl from Junction City?" Before the other kid could answer he'd be on him, "Well, I can't believe she'd marry you cause you're so fuckin' ugly." And everyone in formation would laugh until it petered out. We never cut them off at times like that.

When I was unlucky, I'd get picked for weekend duty and have to babysit the Rifle Company over night. I'd have to police the young privates and make sure the vomit and the beer cans were taken care of in the barracks. Eugene and his friends were never easy, but they were always good natured and never forgot who the sergeant was. When one zagged, another zipped, and as I found out later in life, it was very similar to getting kids ready for school. In the end I'd have to form them up into a drunken semblance of a squad to holler at them before leaving them to their laughter and sleep.

Every six months or so some sergeant major or a colonel somewhere thought it would be a good idea to have a brigade-sized run. At seven in the morning the three and a half thousand or so soldiers from first brigade would form up in a long snaking line. The formation took up the entire road and when the Brigade Commander said go, off we all went. A very slow five miles later and we'd be back at the company releasing the men to shower and change for work. It was always tedious.

To make these things more exciting for everyone, company first sergeants would send privates off on missions to steal some other unit's guidon. This head boy—as they'd say at Eton—would steal the seven or eight-foot pike right out of the hands of another unit's head boy and off he'd go trying not to get caught and knocked around.

Well, at some point in the summer of '05 we had a brigade run. I heard later that the first sergeant had pulled Eugene into his office the night before and, speaking of himself in the third person, said some version of the following: "Look private, the first sergeant's not exactly telling a private he should go and steal the dirty tankers guidon, but if some hooah mother fucker of a private did, well, he'd always be on the first sergeant's good side."

The next morning, after about three and a half miles, while the chubby tankers were getting winded, a beaming, flashing-eyed streak, barely five feet off the ground sped out from a bend in the road, slammed into the tanker head boy, ripped the flag and its phony pike from the kid's hands and took off. He sprinted through several company areas, through parking lots, and around the motor pool. He hurtled past the PX until he reached the 16th Infantry battalion area. He sped on short legs to the Alpha company office and burst, heaving, into the platoon area where he hid the yellow flag emblazoned with a tank. Within a quarter of an hour we were finishing up and stretching outside the company when two tanker first sergeants, their guidon, and PFC Eugene Harmon stormed out the back of our building and past our gaggle of soldiers. The cheers from our boys overrode the instructions being given by the platoon sergeants. They were doubled over anyway and looking at one another and laughing. Our first sergeant, chest puffed and back arched, smiled at his two counterparts from 1-34 armor as they led our favorite eighteen-year-old across the battalion headquarters to meet with both our sergeant major and their own.

Eugene spent that workday polishing the trophy cases and medals the armor unit had displayed in its battalion headquarters. He did a lot of extra push-ups too. ("Don't throw me in the briar patch!") He polished pictures of Shermans in frozen France in 1944 and framed photos of tanks crunching through brush in Vietnam. He shined the glass over the pictures of the Abrams tanks, moving in columns and speeding across the desert in Iraq.

Our first sergeant retrieved Eugene at the end of the day. He led him to our headquarters where our sergeant major promptly gave him a battalion coin. I'm not sure but I think the first sergeant bought Eugene and his buddies a couple cases of beer too. He made them promise to sleep in and skip PT the next morning.

We received orders for a deployment shortly after that, maybe a week, and so we began ramping up to head overseas. Brigade runs and parade ground bullshit immediately disappeared as we prepared to go to war, most likely in Iraq. We raided fake town after fake town. Kicked in innumerable doors. Assaulted Camp Funston time and again with the Bradleys pulling over-watch. Shipped-in Iraqis played street vendors and Imams that harried us in an effort to approximate what even a simple patrol is like overseas. It seemed realistic to those of us that hadn't been there yet, but afterwards, after being there, it was obvious that the only way to be prepared for combat is to be there, smelling it, and not fighting it but taking it on and into ourselves for consumption. Before that, the best you can do is to make sure the boys know everything besides what it is actually like. Make sure they know every weapon system and radio and how to call for fire and drop burning, poisoned shards of steel on the other guy. Make sure the boys can carry their shit, and their buddies' shit, for days on end. Sleep in the cold. Put on a tourniquet, plug a hole, fix a gun truck, and blow a door off its hinges. Make them feel mean. Make them miss their families so they have something to kill for. Once they're over there they'll fight to get home, and they'll fight for each other. They won't have to be told to get mean, over there we're all mean, even the sweet boys are tigers. We marched for miles in the pre-dawn, doubling down on our conditioning. We weren't made to look good. Instead, we looked like rope, dragged through uniforms, booted, carrying weapons and ammo and batteries and water and every other goddamn thing. Eugene was ecstatic.

We'd been in the field on a training mission for a few days when it happened. The bullet entered Eugene's face in the lower left cheekbone. The hole was small and there wasn't a ton of blood at first. The bullet tumbled through his head in a tenth of a second and made a smacking, popping noise when it came out the left side of the back of his head, near where the spine joins with the skull. He fell as though someone pulled all of the bones from his body, collapsing onto his back.

I heard the shot and came around the tent to see what happened. Even if I hadn't heard it, it was obvious something terrible was going on. A kind of smell, or vibration, is emitted into the atmosphere with these things. There's a dread that mushrooms out from the violence itself. It causes that hiccoughing breathing that lasts for a second. Once people are in combat, they begin to react instantly to the sound of gunfire or the thud of a mortar being launched-gritted teeth waiting for the impact-or the smack of a 107 Chinese rocket as it slams into the earth. But this awful thing, Eugene being shot, happened in Kansas, before he ever had a chance to see Iraq, or Afghanistan, or Africa. We were training up. We were practicing at war.

After the day's range time the boy's squad leader, my boss, had neglected to eject a round from his weapon. He dropped the magazine, pocketed it, but instead of racking the bolt and clearing the chamber he simply walked off the squad live fire range with a bullet sitting on the bolt face ready to go. The lieutenant did not check the staff sergeant's weapon out of professional courtesy even though it's policy, and fucking good sense, to clear everyone's weapon as they leave the range.

The accident happened at dusk. We were eating dinner chow, sitting amongst the tents, on the grass, smoking and preparing all our night vision gear, and lasers, and talking about the exercise that was coming.

The squad leader had left his weapon near his bunk—this was also an unheard of mistake—and went to check on his guys, which wasn't. He'd never been overseas and didn't have the instinctual, habitual reflex of constantly carrying his rifle with him, stroking it, cleaning it, checking it. So, there it sat, next to the cot, one 5.56 x 45mm bullet loaded in the chamber, waiting.

I was eating when it happened. I rounded the tent and there was Eugene. The first person I'd seen shot, the little hole in his cheek, the little stream of blood that rivuletted out of it, and the widening, pumping of blood from the back of his head directly into the grass and dirt in between the tents.

Our medic crashed through the crowd of people and began performing on the boy. He did this automatically and didn't hesitate to start working on Eugene as we all gawked and tried to figure out what had just happened. He moved methodically and quickly despite the violence of the dying boy. Another medic appeared by his side bandaging the boy's head. They'd been in Habbaniyah together, the two docs. The first medic had Eugene's shirt ripped open and was performing chest thrusts and mouth to mouth. He threw all of his weight down onto Eugene as he compressed the boy's small chest, and I thought every rib would break. Doc fought for minutes to save that boy. But in the end, the tiny steel bullet that had tumbled through his brain was it. That was the only thing that won the day.

A year later, after a deployment to the Horn of Africa, I left Ft. Riley. I joined another unit, one leaving for Afghanistan. More people were shot, this time overseas away from their homes, sometimes shattered, sometimes just left there, torn up and dead like a grotesque dog on the road. Tongues out, teeth bared, missing hands, and dead. Eugene died like that. He was fucking around with one of his buddies and so he was dead. He'd been fucking around instead of eating, or prepping, or smoking. It seems they'd been "clearing rooms," from tent to tent, had grabbed the squad leader's weapon, clicked off the safety, pad of the finger, squeeze of the trigger, and in a flash, and with incredible violence, he was gone.

We escorted the body home that fall of '05. He came from Indiana, a few miles from its border with Kentucky and Illinois. A tiny town with rolling hills and the last of the autumn leaves falling onto the roads. It was raining that weekend and the town was dreary, muddy, and the red-brown leaves stuck to our tires. Then the road would wind and turn suddenly and lead to a beautiful vista or copse of trees. The lieutenant, our platoon sergeant, the chaplain, and our squad were there to lay the body to rest with our best uniforms and berets and muddy shoes. The squad leader did not go. The private who shot him didn't go either; he was also in custody.

My friend Tim flew ahead early with the body. He was Eugene's team leader. He was there with the family when they opened the casket. The army had neglected to wash the dirt from Eugene's face. Before he died, we'd been in the field for several days and he hadn't showered or anything. His face was waxy, and seemed airbrushed somehow, and the army hadn't washed the dirt from his face. Tim started crying, as did Eugene's mother. He told me that he held her as Eugene's father took a wet handkerchief and washed the dirt from his son's face. Tim couldn't look at the father, he only held Eugene's mother and wept with her. He'd become The Army and felt as though any ills done by the giant organization were on him. Tim had won the bronze star for valor because of stuff he'd done in Iraq the year before. He'd been forced into the army by a judge somewhere in central Kansas four years before that. He was a father, and a husband, and he'd been a killer for over a year by then. He wept with Mrs. Harmon until the crying ended. Eugene's father took him by the shoulder and told him it wasn't his fault. He told Tim that he had served and knew how it was. It wasn't Tim's fault, or my fault, or Eugene's buddies' fault, but that it was The Army's fault.

The truth though, is that it wasn't "The Army's" fault. It was that squad leader's fault. It was the lieutenant's fault for not clearing that squad leader's weapon as we left the exercise. It was his friend's fault: the other private, this one already a combat vet who had been in the invasion in '03, who had shot their son in the face out of negligence. He was supposed to know the ropes, and yet he still picked up an unattended weapon, and fucked around, and pulled the trigger. It was all our fault for not being more aware. And this teenager, this man's boy, was dead before he ever set foot in Afghanistan or Iraq or wherever.

After my second deployment I got out of the army. I felt my luck had run its course and I wanted to see my kids grow up. I get the news through the rumor mill, though. The young man that had pulled the trigger spent a few years at Leavenworth and was now in commercial fishing somewhere in the Gulf of California. His other friend, one of the boys in the barracks and on the gun team, had done a few deployments and had then been stationed in Alaska. He was out walking along the highway one weekend. He had been walking outside of the base up there at Ft. Rich. He was stopped by the police and was almost shot dead there and then. He was walking down the highway with a pump-action shotgun, stinking fucking drunk and yelling at the cars that drove by. The coppers didn't light him up as they were used to working by the base, but instead they got him to lay down the shotgun and get in the patrol car. A couple days later he was in the barracks and put a Glock 23 into his mouth and that was that. I heard this story after getting home from Afghanistan.

The squad leader whose negligence led to all this had been put in Leavenworth for less time than the kid who'd pulled the trigger. He's since gotten out and continued life as a farmer in the northwest. This was really the only mistake I ever saw him make. The same goes for the private. They were good soldiers. Usually, bad mistakes are caught before something like this happens. The amount of bad luck that went into each fuck up leading to Eugene's death is astounding. It is hard to believe when I think about how seriously most of the guys took their jobs. Almost-made life and death mistakes usually end in a shudder and a promise to whomever that it wouldn't happen again, a promise to move on. But this isn't always the case. Sometimes the unseen takes hold of these things, and the trickster gods force them into being. Instead of sitting on his bunk and cleaning his rifle and realizing there's a goddamned round in the chamber, realizing how close he came to disaster, before exhaling with wide eyes and disbelief, the squad leader's attention is turned to something else and he doesn't clean his weapon, doesn't find the round on the bolt face, and the whole series of shitty luck is set in motion.

These days we don't really get together much. A couple of my friends from Afghanistan see one another and teach civilians how to shoot. Some of the other ones live and work in the mountains out west. They never wanted to leave them, I guess. When we all get together, we immediately start drinking and carrying on and the blood starts to rush and creak through the old pipes. We laugh and shit-talk and hug. But all the old bad shit is there too. Perhaps it's just that I like being the only fucked up wild card in the room these days, genteelly teaching a bunch of ne'er do well high schoolers. They have blinders on, and it kind of helps keep mine on too. With the other vets though, the reserves of rage come back out fueled by the booze and the five or six of us middle aged forklift drivers, waiters, CPAs, firemen and other normalized professionals are only a sour word from burning something down.

Being with them is like seeing yourself in old Dorian's picture. Usually nondescript and sometimes-a-little-pudgy men that, when the picture's shade gets pulled back, see only gnarled, furious, animals flapping their wings over dinner. Once this Djinn is out of the box, he brings back Eugene, and Kenny, and Brent, and Chris, and Cody, and Jason and all the other boys that were splayed open by bullets or half melted by explosives or even crushed by flipped armored vehicles, breathing their last breaths in dirt and mud like the trampled Romans at Cannae, unable to see that they were already surrounded and were unable to do anything about it.

WESTERN AND ARMITAGE

THE MAN SAT ON THE STREET with his back against the rear tire on the driver's side of the car. His arm was tangled, I think, in the mechanism behind the wheel and his head was bleeding and smashed in one place. He was dead, or dying at least, and looked like a fiend sitting there with his mouth open. People slowed down as they passed and the waiter from the Cuban diner on the corner was in the street trying to direct traffic and call the police at the same time. I stopped and parked and went out to help. The driver paced in front of the car, looking at the man intertwined with his Toyota saying he had crossed too late without looking and ran right into the side of his car. The man's wallet had flown several yards into the intersection and cars wouldn't stop for me to get it. Eventually there was a red light and I darted out and picked it up. A young man carrying a skateboard and his friend with a mass of curly hair sticking out from under a Bulls cap came running up.

They had kind eyes and wondered how they could help. They looked at the waiter and I for instruction and I remembered I wasn't a kid anymore and pushing fifty. The waiter talked to the cops as they sped towards the intersection from somewhere to the southeast, probably Wicker Park. We could hear the sirens get louder while I directed the two younger men to stop traffic. Most of the cars listened. It's a lot to ask at the end of the day. I looked at the ID and at the man. He wasn't yet thirty, and he wouldn't ever be. The waiter found the man's phone, it flew all the way to the sidewalk on the other side of Western Avenue and cracked. He wanted to hand it all to the police.

Once the police and the ambulance arrived, the four of us looked at one another, shook hands, and parted. "Hey man, be safe." "Have a good one." And so on. The veil had been pulled back into place. I climbed back into the car and took a side street and then an alley to avoid the mess.

LIFE IN THE COLONIES

REUBEN RAN THE BAR at LaFlours hotel and resort outside of San Ignacio. He was friendly, around thirty, and liked to tell stories with the customers. He became animated when he told us about the store he wanted to build, with the restaurant in the back, as he poured drinks for the guests who had just walked in.

He pulled plans for the place from his wallet and laid them on the bar showing us around the store with his finger on the paper. It was written in pencil and smudged around the edges, the lines dark and then graying as they had bled and sweat in his wallet.

"If I can provide people with a cheap, clean place, in between the two towns, I will make a killing," Reuben said.

Maria and I smiled. It was our second day in Belize and our second evening with Reuben at the bar.

A tall, white man came in and bellied up to the bar next to us. He was sunburned, late middle-aged, and his mustache reminded me of pictures of British soldiers in the Boer War.

"Are you boring the guests again, Rueben?" In one movement, Reuben put the plans back in his wallet and then into his back pocket.

Reuben said something we couldn't understand, and the older man laughed.

"What was that?" I asked.

"He's speaking pidgin, it's English," the man said.

Reuben and the man laughed again and said something to one another that sounded like insults. The man turned to us, still laughing. "Do you mind if I sit?"

"No, go ahead." Maria said. He pulled up a stool and looked out, off the terrace of the LaFlours hotel, into the private lives of the birds and insects that lived in the trees above the river and the jungle floor.

"Are you from London?" I asked.

"Oh, thank god! Almost everyone from your country thinks I'm an Australian."

We shook hands, and he said his name was George Taylor.

The four of us talked about the jungle lodge and its amenities. We drank the daiquiris Reuben made for us. He kept his below the bar, but every now and again he'd look around and then take a drink.

"I'm good friends with the LaFlours." Taylor said. "I grew up with the old man, so when I could help him, I did. I'm the groundskeeper here."

"I'm sorry to hear about his passing." Maria said.

"Thanks, Love. Cheers." He took a pull on the Belikin beer Reuben had placed in front of him. "They pay me in trade. I take home orchids to sell in London. And they pick up my bar tab when I'm here."

We spoke for an hour longer about Belize and about each other's countrymen and sports while Reuben listened, grinning, and chiming in every few minutes. Otherwise, he watched and listened for the punch line as though he knew when it would arrive. At ten it was time to close the bar. We were all waking up with the sun. George turned to us as Reuben was cleaning up the blender, "How 'bout the two of you come on a tour of the garden tomorrow, on me?"

"Yeah, thanks," I said. "We'd love to."

We said our goodbyes and Maria and I walked up the path to our lodge. We kissed looking at the stars from the screened porch and went to bed. The ceiling fan was drowned out by the deafening blackness and the clamor of unseen animals.

The next morning George Taylor showed us his gardens. He had cut them from the jungle itself and let the jungle thrive where he wanted it, where Mr. LaFlours and he had planned it. Controlled wilderness. That was the English Garden. It looked like a huge cottage garden in Chichester, or Portsmouth, on the English Channel. It'd been constructed on a grand scale. Stretching over rolling, hilly acres it had a real Mayan hut, hundreds of trees, flowers, two ponds, birds, insects, observation decks, and Mr. LaFlour's remains, at the highest point, marked with a cross. There are four dogs and a gimpy, drunk security guard that Taylor disallowed from carrying real shotgun shells. He beamed while giving us the tour and we told him it was a wonderful place.

"It is, isn't it?" he said proudly.

"Yes, it's very beautiful." Maria said.

"Not as beautiful as you." He said to Maria and winked at me.

"Why don't you give the guard his shells?" I asked.

"He's a drunk, and a Belizean. Which means he's lazy and he'll shoot someone accidentally."

"Lazy?"

"Well, Betty Laflours hires locals, which is good. But when I'm not here, they don't do much. When I head back to London, I leave instructions to the guard and the landscapers. They don't follow what I tell them to do. I tell them to cut twice a week, they don't cut until I return. I tell them to weed and to spray, I tell them to mend the fences, to build supports for the new plants. The list is endless. They don't do any of it."

He turned and pointed towards the hills in the west at the border with Guatemala.

"They're cutting down their hardwood forests to raise cattle for quick cash. Slash and burn, you know."

"Oh."

"Their idea of hard work is different from ours. That's why they're so poor."

I could tell Maria wanted to argue with him. She began to say something, but Taylor had already started walking towards the orchid house. I touched her arm and she looked at me and rolled her eyes. Despite all this, we loved the tour and even Taylor too, if only for what he'd built there in the jungle, and because he was very much his own man.

The tour ended at ten. Maria collected our things from the bungalow while I had the kitchen pack some muffins and bottled water in a basket. A dog followed us as we walked down the path from the lodges, through the giant legs of the deck that started on the hill, one hundred feet up. The deck jutted out from the hillside, wooden poles gradually lengthening the farther out it stretched over the jungle. We trudged, basket and dog in tow, through the jungle to the river and the tiny beach at its edge. Reuben had left a canoe with paddles and jackets sitting on the bank. It wasn't tied up, but sat, leaning on its side in the sand, one curved end in the water. There was a letter in the boat from Reuben. It was addressed to Maria and gave directions to the butterfly house exhibit at Clarissa Falls, a few miles downriver.

The Macal River wasn't so different from the Cuyahoga in the summer, as it meanders south of Cleveland through the metro-parks. Both were serene and there were herons that skimmed the top and ripples where the fish broke the surface. It was warm and alive. And then the river would bend, and you'd realize you were in Central America, on a river that cut its own vein through the jungle's rocks and colors. Trees grew out over the river in a canopy, in some places perpendicular to the rock walls that always seemed ready to fall in on the canoe. They'd shed their skin many times over the generations they'd perched there, filling the banks with rocks and dirt. We were afraid of piranha, but there weren't any. We were afraid of alligators too, but they didn't live there either. The forest was feminine, screaming to Juno and Anahita about Virginity; and then birth, and rebirth, and then silence, the total silence of a still river at noon. Bushes rumble, Howler monkeys scream from half a mile off, a dip in the water where something you'd never see went back under. The jungle. Color and alive and always in motion, shifting with the breeze and the heat. Finally, Maria went swimming. She dove in, halfway between LaFlours and Clarissa Falls.

Along the river there was quiet and then shacks on tiny stilts where little, dark-skinned boys fished off rocks or swung from the trees into the water. Then there were jungle lodges and fishing outposts. Every mile or so, two or three canoes tied to tiny docks, unguarded and silent, drifted with each other back and forth in the current. We paddled along looking for Clarissa Falls. Maria wanted to see the butterfly exhibit. She'd seen it online and had been planning the stop for weeks. Reuben's letter endeared him more to her and we spoke often of him as we paddled down river. Finally, after three miles, we saw the yellow and red canoes of Clarissa Falls and pulled to the dock, wedging our canoe between theirs and tying it to the metal cleat.

The bank from the river was steep and she had to stop often because her shoes didn't have backs and kept coming off. We took it slow; it was already nearing a hundred degrees and it was only noon. Her shoes finally came off and she balanced herself on the wooden planks alongside the path as we climbed the embankment.

The Butterfly House was no bigger than a two-car garage. It had mesh walls, wood framing, and an official looking young man in khaki standing at the entrance. As we neared, he escorted another white couple from its gate and motioned to the salesgirls who stood nearby with T-shirts in a cardboard box.

The man in khaki looked tired. He sweat into his collar and wiped his forehead with a handkerchief he kept in his belt. He was handsome, though, and used to charming people. He tried smiling and led us through the door without charging us.

The butterflies were all flying sticks and colors. They were flowers that had uprooted and taken to the air, dipping and rising as they flew. Sense of direction constantly breaking down and coming to once again as they jerked themselves on silky wings from lover to perch to the melon tray where they ate rotten fruit. The guide said there were scores of them.

"Say hello to the Blue Morpho," he said.

"Hello," said Maria. I nodded and tried a bow. The guide didn't laugh.

"They are beautiful?" he asked.

"Yes, very." They were a shade of blue I couldn't recognize. It was patterned on their wings in splotches. It is an iridescent blue, a violet almost, that when in motion appears like streaks of color in front of your eyes.

"What shade of blue is that?" I said, "It's amazing." The guide only nodded and smiled. He shrugged. He'd heard all this before, and it was very hot. Sometimes the jerky paths of the insects would veer towards Maria and I and we would shift out of the way like boxers. She threw a jab at one but the guard just looked at her and then leaned down to change the melon trays.

"They're territorial, you know," the guard said from the melon trays. "They tear each other apart if another one crosses their lines.

Very odd, isn't it? In here?"

"It is," said Maria.

I looked at her and jerked my head towards the door. She nodded.

"Well, thank you sir."

The guide looked up at us, "Could you be careful on your way out, I don't want to let any escape."

"Of course."

Maria stopped. "Excuse me."

"Yes?" The guide answered her from his knees.

"What kind are these brown ones, these butterflies up here in the corner?"

The guide cocked his head and looked at her, his eyes wider than before.

"Oh, well, those are Blue Morpho too, the blue is only on the inside. When they aren't flying, or showing off, they close their wings. Everything else on them is brown, like the ground, so they can hide from birds and things."

Oh. Thanks," she said. I was holding by the door, ready to make the dash into the corridor.

I waved to the young man who waved back and returned to cleaning up the feeding area, sweating onto the melons he was cutting into slices and placing on the trays.

We walked back down the path to the hillside, and then down through brush to the river. I untied the canoe and pushed us off, climbing in as it scraped against the rocks by the shore. A dog from the dock dove in the water and followed us out for a few yards and then lost interest and began barking at the birds on the riverbank.

We paddled for another hour, stopping now and then to swim or take a picture. Traffic on the river increased as we neared San Ignacio, there were other canoes and more children were in the water waving to us as we paddled by. We passed the suspension bridge and pulled up to the cement dock. Reuben and another man stood waiting to haul us out of the river. "How did you like the trip?"

"Great," I said.

"Did you stop to see the butterflies?"

"We loved them," Maria said. I nodded.

"Do you need a hand putting this up there?" I asked him and looked to the top of the truck Reuben and his partner had driven into town.

"No. Don't worry about it, man." He patted me on the shoulder. "Your car is up the street that way, past the church." He pointed, and then, "Do you need directions to the ruins?"

"No Reuben, I think we've got everything. Thanks."

"See you later guys."

We left Reuben and the other man and walked up past the car and the church and into the heart of San Ignacio. Five blocks of dirt and brick road infused with corrugated tin-roofed bars, restaurants, and shack homes on stilts. We ate on a patio and watched the people speed by in pick-ups that would careen past the restaurant, take the turn too fast, and scrape the ground as they went by. American tourists and Rastafarians backpacked through the town.

Maria wanted to see the ruins, so we walked to the truck and circled San Ignacio a few times, looking for the Western highway to the Guatemalan border and the Xunantunich ruins. By three we had found the ferry where a Mayan with a wide-brimmed hat motioned us onto the pontoon. A younger man at the winch began cranking us across. We had an hour, the man said, so we pulled up around the hill and walked through the ruins. We took pictures from the top of the pyramid and pretended to play ball in the overgrown stadium.

We took the long way home through low and winding hills. The road follows the Macal River around and over the mounds and through the little villages on its way back to San Ignacio. It was beautiful and paved and so we took our time, the windows open as the early dusk came on. That was western Belize in March, early sunsets and still rivers.

Neither of us were hungry after the driving and the heat and the river. She slept on the bed as I dozed in the hammock, reading about Lewis and Clark and the Mandan Sioux. At seven we dressed and headed down the path to the bar and Reuben and George Taylor. George told us about Belizean rum, and how he thought it was the best in the world. Later we tried One Barrel with its almost Butterscotch taste, and liked it better, especially when you mixed it with pineapple. But that night, on the terrace, he force-fed us Durley's and Belikin and Reuben made Piña Coladas. By nine the four of us were talking louder and laughing at everything. We'd forgotten about the birds and spiders and about the six-foot iguana, who lives on the branches off the terrace end of the deck. We were concerned only with people then, and the stories of the four of us in a bar.

Before the kitchen closed Reuben went and made us sandwiches, ham and Swiss and roast beef. When he left, George leaned in close, and in the way of telling a secret, "Was he telling you about the store when I came in last night?"

"Reuben?" I asked.

"Yeah."

"Yes, he told us," Maria said, "He's wonderful, isn't he? I think he's on to something."

George smiled at Maria. "He'll never leave, Hon."

"What do you mean, he'll never leave?"

"He won't do it," he said, still smiling. "He's just dreaming out loud. He can play a part with the two of you, he won't see you again."

"Oh, come on," I said. "He showed us the plans and the costs and everything. He even carries them around in his goddamn wallet."

George sat back in his chair and shook his great, gray and pink head. I could tell Maria thought he was being mean. I looked at her and shrugged.

"I offered to take him to London to work for me. That was a year ago. Betty Laflours even offered to pay for his ticket. He didn't go. He's got connections in New York and Chicago too."

"That's what he told us."

He took a drink and looked around the side of the terrace and then back at us. "Reuben's part of this place, and nothing from this place ever gets out. Maybe to Belize City, or Belmopan, but nowhere else. And as he gets older it will be easier to make excuses than to actually do something about it. I'm sorry to be the one to tell you," and he clapped a hand on Maria's knee, "but it's true."

"He seemed so sure though," she said and shifted from under his hand.

"He's a good boy, Reuben, but he couldn't even if he was serious about it. The people here don't have the stones to leave, I mean they're scared."

"They don't have the money to leave," Maria said and frowned at George.

"It's more than that, and it's more than just being 'small town.' Reuben's got the little baby after all."

"What?" Maria moved in closer.

"Yeah, lives with its mum, while he stays out here six days a week. He takes them his money, and then swimming or something, on Mondays."

"He didn't tell us."

We didn't say much after that. We sat and drank and listened to the radio until Reuben got back with the sandwiches. They were large, with thick bread and mayonnaise that tasted good and fresh. We swallowed it with the beer. We were leaving the next morning for the coast and a puddle-jumper to the Keys. George made us promise to rise early and meet him for coffee and the bird watching hour at dawn. We said good night to them both and then headed up the path, through the jungle, to our room and the dancing and screaming of the beasts on the roof and the treetops nearby.

The next morning Reuben caught us at a dead run. I heard him yelling first and then saw him in the mirror, running, his backpack bouncing up, almost over his shoulders as he leapt over potholes in the long driveway. We stopped. He reached the car and leaned on the door, breathing heavily. I had no idea how long he'd been running after us. The LaFlours' dogs that had been chasing him gave up and began searching for something in the weeds.

"Hey guys." He was smiling. He wiped his face with a towel from his pocket. "Can you drop me in town?"

"Of course, Reuben, my boy."

"How's your head?" he asked me.

"However it is, Reuben, is your fault," I said.

He laughed at this and he climbed into the backseat.

"I'm going to see my family. It's been a week."

"I bet you're a good father, Reuben." Maria said.

He only nodded and looked from her to me. As we made our way to town Reuben was quiet and stared out of the window, now and then drying off with his towel. Twenty minutes later we were pulling through the narrow, dirt streets of San Ignacio, around the roundabout, and dropped him at the police station.

"Well, thanks for the ride guys. It was nice knowing you," he said.

I handed him a piece of paper with my address and number on it. "Listen, Reuben, if you make it to Chicago drop me a line. I'll take you out. Show you a good time. Okay?"

Reuben took the paper with my number on it but wouldn't look me in the eye. We shook hands. "Do you know where you're going?" he asked.

"Yes. Thanks."

"Bye, honey. Tell your family we said hello," Maria said.

And with that Reuben did look up at us. He smiled again and then shut the door and walked in front of our car, across the street and down an alley.

Days later, a short haired mutt perched himself next to me. I hadn't noticed him until he shook sand and water in my face, and I realized I was back on the dock, at the Split, where people swam on the island. It was a kind of lagoon, between the halves of Caye Caulker, cut asunder by a hurricane forty years before. One could sit at the Split, on the peopled side, and stare across to the other island, where the birds lived. A wooded swampy key where cats, of all things, hunted between the twisted roots, diving onto fish that stayed in the shade.

The mutt's mouth was open in a smile and he looked at me with sideways eyes. He was only a foot away and covered in sand, dirty like the other mutts on the island. He was happy though, and panting, his eyes shining, his tongue out. I noticed Maria had just taken a picture of me and was laughing.

"You just made a friend."

Oh. Hey pooch," I said and scratched his head.

"Where'd you go? I've been staring at you for days now." She looked at the book I was holding. It wasn't open.

"Off in my head, I guess. Do you want to go swimming?"

She put the camera down and dove into the water. It was the color of sun-bleached limes that afternoon and I watched her swim around in front of me for a few minutes, chasing fish like a little girl in the shallows, before I dove in after her.

NEW ORLEANS

FOUR MEN SAT AT A BALCONY TABLE overlooking Magazine Street. They'd been at it for a day and a half, and had twenty-four hours before their flight back to Chicago and fatherhood and forty-something. They had ruddy skin and were pie-eyed and wobbled a little heading up and down the stairs. Every couple of minutes the men would pause and watch the rain that had been falling all morning before one of them launched into another bit they'd been working on for twenty years. They told stories and laughed at each other.

"Tom Sawyer is a drunk."

"Oh lord. Here we go."

They all started laughing.

"You know what," said Mark, "everyone wants to be Huck Finn, but you're Tom Sawyer, man."

"No way."

"Yup. Just keep painting away on that fucking fence man."

"Thanks, Mark."

They all laughed again.

"And now nothing is how you thought it would be and you're drinking yourself into oblivion with me and these other idiots."

"Well, at least I'm not a quitter."

"No. You're not a quitter."

The waitress dropped off another pitcher of beer. Two of the men lit cigarettes, blowing the smoke out into the rain that fell just out of reach of the balcony. They poured drinks and looked out onto the street. A disheveled man yelled up at them from under an awning on the corner. It was hard to hear him over the rain.

"What?" Mark yelled down. The man crossed Magazine Street and stood under the balcony where the sidewalk met the road. He cupped his hands.

"God do shit a poyson ain't supposed tuh do." He nodded at the men afterwards and made his way back across the street to the restaurants along the block and their awnings.

The four men laughed and talked about faery tales and how only the good stuff hides under the bridge or visits at night when maybe you were only half asleep and could not tell if it was really happening. They were drunk but really cruising along and thinking clearly.

"Hey, Tom Sawyer."

"Yes, Mark?"

"How'd you convince your principal to let you out of the classroom?"

"I pretty much told him I'd quit if I didn't get out."

"And he fell for that?"

"Well, not him. His sidekick, the Unterführer, he's a good guy and a drinking buddy and vouched for me."

"No shit. He knows you, doesn't he?"

"Well, I know where all the bad stuff is hidden. And who fucked who and when. And I know how none of the grades are real." Tom Sawyer paused, "You know. Old guy magic."

They laughed and drank and waited for the rain to let up to head out and trek down the boulevard. It still misted, and they had most of a pitcher left. The bum had retreated back into the neighborhood and they didn't see him again until they made their way back down the other side of the Garden.

FEE WAIVER

IN THE END, he thought, all day-jobs seemed to turn into that factory gig he'd had in Miamisburg outside of Dayton back in '93. He drove there in the morning and sat at a table surrounded by other tables and bales of paper. The stacks of paper were taller than he was. There were pushcarts and balers and the full-time workers. They were mostly Appalachian. The men, no matter what age, were lean and strong and smoked outside at every break. The women were friendly but acted as if he were a foreigner. The table he worked at was larger than one person needed. There was a slot in the top of the table and stacks of metal rails in a box next to him on the ground. There was also a stack of cardboard pages. He placed the metal rail in the slot, then fit the cardboard letter into the slot on top of the metal rail. He stomped on a foot pedal and just like that, another ballot came into being. This gets old after half an hour and that was just the early morning. The Appalachians didn't seem to mind how monotonous it all was, though that couldn't be true. He had been too young to try to figure out why. At the end of the assignment, he knew one thing, not sitting all day was better than sitting all day.

A few years later, he and his buddies moved to Chicago. He got a temp job in the vault of a bank a block or two from the Art Institute somewhere on Monroe. In '96 the CTA still took dollar bills, and bag after bag were brought down the stairs and through the vault archway and laid at his feet. He spent eight hours a day pulling the dollar bills from the bags, unfolding them, and then placing them face up to be counted by one of those clicky machines that counts dollar bills. He wasn't left alone with the money, obviously, so he and two old ladies sat unfolding bills until lunch, had a break, and then again until quitting time. It was hard to get the filth off his hands after handling thousands of dollar bills. He worried about getting sick and keeping his hands clean, but he had to ride the Blue Line from Monroe back to Division street. They'd just get filthy again holding one of those lukewarm handrails anyway. From the Algren fountain he took the bus to Campbell and the metal Puerto Rican flag that bent up over Division street. He washed up in his dirty apartment. He did this for exactly three days until he stopped going to the vault and stayed in bed with a fever. The temp agency called his roommate. His buddy made it a few days longer than he did. He got sick too. These kinds of jobs made up the better part of a decade.

This was before the Army, before being married, before children. It was before owning things. It was before being disillusioned. He knew something was up though, even back then. There was a nagging sense that something wasn't right. Maybe a real feeling in the guts that these jobs, these enormous wastes of time, were just different kinds of death. Or maybe it was all a joke being played on everyone. He wasn't sure. The summers and autumns he'd spent landscaping and cutting grass were the fondest memories he had. Being outside all day and working with his body had been a tonic. That was the real magic.

These revelations about the necessity of work and trying to do something meaningful were understood about as well as a twenty-five-year-old American white kid in that decade understood things. Well-read and angry, but ultimately he was without anything beyond angst.

He could rebel in the way other young artist types rebelled. It was real, but it was safe. He could peacock in a neighborhood full of peacocks, read Dostoevsky and Miller and Hamsun, drink too much, stay up all night, go to important rock shows and festivals. He could sleep with as many women as possible or try whatever anyone put in front of him.

But it was all safe and at worst he'd have a hangover, or a broken heart, or a busted lip. Maybe lose a friend. But real rebellion, the kind that has the anvil tied to your ankle, can only come when you have some part of you to lose. When losing that thing makes you desperate and murderous enough to consider killing yourself or someone else. This is what he saw looking back at him in the mirror as he turned forty-five sitting in that fucking classroom getting ignored. If he did something radical now, there would be consequences and he could get pulled down into the deep.

He'd asked the principal if there was anything besides teaching that he could do without leaving the school. A week or two later the college counselor quit, and he inherited the job. His days became more occupied. His hands began hurting from the typing. He gained ten pounds by Christmas and his back started to hurt. But he was less frustrated with the students. They began to seem like human beings again. He went back to coaching. He went back to patting them on the back and giving side hugs. His job was getting the kids in college and because he again saw them as individuals, the teacher was able to enjoy making their lives better.

The first year went well, as well as could be expected at any rate, but by the end something was eating at him. The second year went a little better, but the nagging feeling was still there. He had friends that didn't think about these things. Or at least, they didn't bother about them. He was jealous of them. They had been able to stay in the classroom and not worry about existential calamities. His buddies in the Army were like that too, but he liked them better. At least they didn't pretend about the impact they had on the world. They weren't too self-important.

The handshake deal is what really pissed him off. The deal people made with everyone else to believe things were happening that weren't happening. The deal people made with themselves to pretend. Some pretended to care about their work, or what others thought about them. Others pretended that being there every day mattered. There was no magic in their thinking, only a foggy lie that they stuck to for dear life. And worst of all, they all pretended to know what was best for other peoples' children. And in that way, it was invasive, and it was corrupt.

A large part of his job was preparing kids to apply for college and seeking out financial aid. To do this, the students needed their parents' tax returns. The principal didn't really care if every individual kid hassled his parents for them, but the city sure as hell did. And since they tracked it, the principal had to care. By extension then, so did the teacher. And he was the one telling kids to ask their parents why they hadn't done their taxes. Why couldn't they do this little thing to help their own children. Can you imagine? In this alternate reality all the staff and hangers on act like it's acceptable that the parents don't do what they are supposed to do as productive adult people. The educators shrug their shoulders and bite their lips and feel guilty. They treat them like children and make excuses for adults that don't do the bare minimum. They pretend like it is helpful and normal and not elitist or racist to behave this way.

The state and the universities are in on it too. Illinois gives money to the poor kids like they said they would. The kids fill out the paperwork and then get on average ten or so thousand dollars a year for college. The schools themselves gave the kids money too. The better the grades, or higher the test score, the more money they'd be willing to give a student. The private schools gave a lot in the way of grants, but they were so expensive it didn't really matter. The kids couldn't cover the nut anyway. The bigger schools that weren't going anywhere gave almost nothing unless the kid was exceptionally tall, or fast, or smart. Really smart. The University of Illinois wouldn't give the A student anything. That kid is a dime a dozen down there. You'd need to be exceptional for the U of I to pay your way. Unless the kid was really fast, like I said. They'd never beat the Buckeyes or Penn State without speed, so they still had to try.

So, the kids got ten grand a year from the state. The schools took the money from the state and let the kids on campus. When they failed out during the first semester or couldn't acclimate after a few months away from the city and returned to its separate reality, the school kept the state's money. The kid still got the bill, but was now back at home at nineteen, surrounded by failure, and looking for hourly work. He'd carry that bill for years and by the time he dragged his ass down to a city college or the recruiter's office to learn how to salute, it had compounded. It's not laziness that gets them. It's a belief that nothing one does will matter anyway. It's nihilism. And the city created it. He put the ballot in the metal slot, made sure it was snug, and pressed down on the pedal. Another ballot came to life. It was cynical, and it was obscene.

The kids were told for years to study hard. They were told to ignore the drugs, and the violence, and to abstain. The school stopped really grading English and Math and Physics because it was too hard. The kids would just fail. So, the names were kept the same, but the classes often taught just the ACT. The teachers poured over the questions and explained how they were written. They discussed strategies and the eight comma rules because that was the most frequently tested skill on the test. They did this day in and out like exercise. Most of the kids wouldn't have read The Catcher in the Rye if it were assigned anyway. They simply practiced the test.

The city demands results on the tests. It demands that the students go to college in higher numbers. The grades get inflated in the name of fairness. The kids don't fail, the lowest Fs became 50 percent, and then were cracked in half again. Passing became 20 percent. The teachers worried more about their broken hearts than about math. They don't address the real business. Society and poverty are monolithic, and the school is populated with some below average adults with four-year degrees from Northeastern and National Louis. We bang on about the test. There are four practice tests throughout the year. The teachers give out prizes for improvement. They work the stamper and pile up the ballots. They ignore the greats. Aristotle can't help a kid who can't spell, or is fucking pregnant, or pisses in the back of the classroom, or whips his cock out to show fourteen-year-olds. He can in the movies, but not in real life. If the kids score low, then the school's rating drops and teachers are doubted. Then even less motivated and less intelligent kids come to the school because the rating is lowered and even less gets done. This doesn't seem to make any sense. The problem could be fixed, but really, Rahm didn't send his kids to the city schools. Neither did

Barack. Not even close.

The teacher couldn't leave though. He needed the cheese from CPS. His kids needed insurance, and the condo needed paying for. The Hondas needed gas. He fled to New Orleans with friends once a year and sent his kids to Florida in the summer, so he and the wife could act like they were twenty-five again. A week here, a week there, and the freedom of it fuels the double shifts at the factory. His daughter asked him after school one day, "it seems like people are so unhappy with their jobs. Why do they torture themselves?" The teacher kind of grunted. He didn't answer and hoped that maybe she'd be one of those people who absolutely loves what they do. There was a chance, right? His wife was one of those people. She loved her job. Some of the teachers are like that too. He knew them. They could be spotted a mile away. They are brightly colored and stand out. They teach while everyone else is gray.

ANOTHER GINGER ALE AFTERNOON

THE AFGHAN SOLDIERS WERE LAUGHING and smoking when they walked up to the bomb. They stood over it and kicked at the ground on top of it. One of their sergeants called over an Afghan private and made him start to dig at the bomb with his hands and an entrenching tool. We all held our breath and ducked. We were laughing, and ducking, and smoking and looking at the Afghans with awe and pity. It took a while but finally the private had dug away the rocky ground from around the bomb. It was a silver coffee container filled with homemade explosives. Our lieutenant wouldn't let them just pick it up out of the hole in the road, so the Afghan sergeant collected his men's scarves. They always wore these colorful, dashing scarves. The sergeant tied them together from end to end to make a rope. He attached one end to the bomb and then walked off the dirt road into the wash. The road was two meters or so above the valley floor and he and his men stood there, in the grass, at eye level with the road and the bomb and they began to yank. This went on for a good ten minutes and we loved it. Every time they'd yank on the scarf we'd duck behind a boulder and wait for the blast. But every time the scarf would come loose from the canister and they'd fall into each other, climb the road, reattach the scarf and do it again. This went on for a while until it finally worked, and they pulled it from the ground. Later we could see the coffee container had writ large across its middle the letters "USA." It was apparently from USAID or some other American organization. This wasn't the first one we'd found like this either. It wasn't too big, not like the big, yellow, jug bombs they'd attach to a pressure plate, but big enough. Haj has a sense of irony, for sure.

Back at the Outpost we put the coffee bomb in our UXO pit. I'd carried ordinance there before. Chinese recoilless rifle rounds, unexploded mortar bombs, and belts of Russian ammo were all normal and something you'd expect to collect and put in a big pit that would eventually get the shit blown out of it. They would use everything they could to try to hurt us. In their eyes we were the faceless, the godless, the smiling, the Borg, or the Legions or something. In those valleys there was no Kabul, and there was no Chicago, there were only the stone walls and goat pens, and the people that believed we were there to harm them. They were scared and uneducated and had manipulative people whispering in their ears, telling teenagers to shoot at Americans for fifty bucks, telling them to bury bombs in the roads and under culverts to incinerate the people who trod over them. They didn't tell the teenagers that we'd kill them first and maybe never even see the manipulative ones.

SQUAW ROCK

I WENT HOME FOR A REUNION a couple years ago. That part isn't time travel, but it's the beginning. It was in early October. The leaves had changed, but the grass was still a deep green. The Great Lakes are beautiful at that time of year and I spent much of Saturday morning jogging through the parks along the Chagrin River. It was quiet and the air was crisp. I'd watched my alma mater whip Strongsville the night before, then stopped at a popular restaurant near the hotel and had gotten a little drunk. By the afternoon my old buddy Marcus Antonius called and said we should meet for drinks and watch the Buckeyes. We met at the local hole and started going pretty hard even though we had the reunion a couple hours later. At some point in the conversation a hand rested on my shoulder.

"I thought that was you jogging this morning, Chris. I almost ran you over!" My high school girlfriend was standing next to me, smiling as she hugged me. She looked great and was very professional about the whole thing. And then her hand rested on the back of my neck, and she touched my skin, and I was seventeen again. No one in their forties, despite what they may say, should really feel what it was like to be in love at seventeen or eighteen again. And one should never have it spiked right into a vein all at once. The bar disappeared, and I was back to that time, and I was brash again, and I was shy again, and I wanted to hold her so tightly that she'd die and couldn't ever go away. The whole thing lasted maybe three seconds, but it happened, and it was as real as she was, standing there next to me. She kept her hand there for a beat too long. It was imperceptible, but I knew it. Was she a witch? Was it an accident and she felt it too? I don't know, but I was there in 1990 once again.

Her hand slipped from my neck and I tried to have a conversation with her. I couldn't muster much past a few syllables. She seemed to do fine however, and after a few pleasantries, walked out to meet with her family and leave. I heard Antonius chuckle to his wife that I used to "get with that girl" in his car. I meant to holler at him for being crude, but I still couldn't speak. I got up to go to the bathroom. I passed the front door where she stood, getting a coat on her young son. She looked up at me and smiled and walked out. I sat in the stall for a while waiting for re-entry while a muted Bowie crooned at me from a circle speaker in the wall.

NO TRAVEL RETURNS

HE WOKE UP AND RAN WITH THE DOG. He did this every day. He woke up and he ran with the dog. Then he showered, dressed, and woke up the kids. This happened every day, too. Then he made breakfast for the kids and woke up his wife. This kept happening. He made it happen, this routine. He got them ready for school and then left for work, teaching other children that didn't listen to what he had to say. His wife took their kids to school. Often, they would fight, his wife and he, over little things that had grown large. These little-things-fought-over masked the cavernous things that would implode the life they led. He tried to leave those things alone. The drink helped too. When he was too spun up, always breathing the last minute's breath when he should've been on to the next, the drink helped. He played with the kids and went out with his wife. This all kept happening day in and day out.

The club was dark and lit with torches and had a dirt floor. The wooden handrails and steps were worn smooth. It had been packed with soldiers, embassy kids, mercenaries, and prostitutes for so long that the dirt was hard and didn't rise even when it hadn't rained for weeks. The girl's name was Whitney; the soldiers had no idea why she chose that for her English name. She had very dark skin and was willowy and tall but also curvy and would have been in a different place if she had been born in the States.

Whitney spoke with the sergeant about Kampala while he sat drinking at a wooden table. The men danced with the other girls on the dirt floor.

"At least Edi Amin was honest about who he was," she said, "even with all the people he killed back then. People still disappear now you know; Museveni just lies about it to us...he must have to lie about it to himself too."

When she said this, she was an adult and certain and looked directly into his eyes, without the flirtatious, amusing way she'd bantered with all of them the other times they'd met her and her friends at the club. Later that night, when she was dancing with Mac, the sergeant watched her face as she laughed, grinding on her American suitor, and she was again robotic and like a doll.

He picked the kids up after school. Went home. Did homework with them, walked the dog, and cooked dinner. This happened every day as well. There are only a few hours' worth of living in between picking the kids up and putting them to bed, so the time had to be regimented. They ate, did work, played, and went to bed. Then he and his wife would start drinking and staring at the television, unable to really do much else. He was exhausted, and it was good. The buzzing behind the eyes, the spinning device hurtling through his chest like the little steam engine burned up at Alexandria needed to be slowed. In the old days there could be reading, or more exercise, or discussion, but now, exhausted as he was-as they were-there was only the couch, and the drink, and then sleep.

The old man stood at the gate with the little boy in his arms. Afghan guards let them in, and the lieutenant was rushed to the gate with the doc and one of his medics. The boy was in and out of this world and pale, but around his eyes was red and he had been crying as they walked up to the gate. There was blood on their clothes, and it stained their robes a dirty brown that mixed thick with the dust from the road. When the LT got there the old man stared but could not open his mouth without crying; the boy stared past the strange men to the hillside and sunglassed Americans walking in the background. A man from their village had been angry at some slight to his family, or his goats, or the village, and had caught the boy when he was alone. He'd used a saber and slashed at the boy's hand, severing tendon and some bone, the fat bubbled out from the wound. The men rushed him to the aid station and the doc treated the wound and all the medics took turns trying to cheer up the young boy. Thirty minutes later a Blackhawk landed on the tiny gravel LZ in the front of the outpost and took the boy away. American doctors in Bagram doctors were able to save his hand and fight the infection and two weeks later the Blackhawk returned with the boy and his grandfather. The soldiers thanked them for trusting Americans and sent them back out, across the valley floor to their village and the goats and stone homes.

He showered, dressed, and woke up the kids. This happened every day and it was good. He was whittling away at the bill. This life seemed to be happening faster and the promises that he'd made to the gods, the ones that had kept him alive all these years, seemed to be wearing thin. The other lives, the ones the gods had spared despite being evil or violent or ineffectual, were coming back to him more quickly now, reminding him of the promises he'd made and the things he'd done, and that in the end someone had to ante up. As sure as the sun would rise tomorrow, he knew it was true.

The woman was tall, coltish really, and looked like she was from the Black Sea. She'd been drinking all day and her eyes were alternately glazed and perceptive. There were flashes of violence in them, tremendous violence and anger that scared people that saw them. She was angry with her boyfriend and had taken a cab all the way from Wicker Park to a bar in Pilsen to see him and share with him the violence and betrayal that she felt couldn't be tolerated alone.

He had his back turned when she started hitting him. The woman slammed her fists into his back one after another and all the men and women that stood around the man stepped back in horror. It was as if an odor of violence had been released and pushed the people away from the man getting hit. He turned around and watched her hitting him, now in the stomach and chest. The man put his arms up and out to his sides, looking at the people around him so they knew he wasn't the one doing the hitting. Flames shot from her fists when they hit the man. They'd flare up and then go out, one after another.

Then the woman, her hands were claws, grabbed his face, her nails driving into his cheeks, her fingers white, and bloodless.

"I fucking hate you!" the woman screamed into his face, "I hate you!"

One of the women nearby braved the violence and said to her, "You can't do that in here. You have to get out. Someone kick her out of here."

The man pulled her hands from his face. He was much stronger than she was, but none of that mattered. She'd just taken everything from him. His friends, there were three of them, stood near him and didn't look at him. They looked at one another without speaking. All of the happiness in the room had been pulled into this event. This malice fed on the happiness, burning it up and fueling more malice, and violence, making it even hotter and more intense. If there were a spirit world, one the people could see, it would be all flame and chaos.

There wasn't really a way to bring the man back to himself. He was gone, his friends would have to deal with this, and the room started moving again, trying to create more happiness. The woman was led to the bar where a bartender called a cab. She seemed to shrink, and the flames left her hands and her eyes, and she slumped on a stool at the end of the bar waiting for the cab, drunk, and exhausted. The door behind her opened as people brought the cold and the snow into the room, stomping it from their boots and hair.

He was in his forties now and the dream of running back in time became forefront in his mind. The dream of running home to Ohio: to the parks, and the herons, and football, and the creek that a body could lay in and let the water slowly pour over itself, made him feel that everything could be right if only he could get back to that. Chicago wasn't able to protect him any longer; he needed the old magic, the childhood memories to bathe in, the ones made before anything bad had been done.

The men were laughing when the sergeant got back to the tents.

He'd been talking to the lieutenant and the platoon sergeant and was now heading back to the men. They were laughing and stood in a gaggle. One of the men was yelling at the others. The ones getting yelled at held a slingshot. It was large and made to shoot water balloons very far. The men were bored and not on patrol rotation for another day. They spent their time doing chores and staying busy, but by now, eight months in the deployment, the chores were done quickly, and they had too much time on their hands. The sergeant reached the men, and the argument, and the angry soldier who was yelling.

"Look sergeant. Look." He pointed to the hillside twenty meters away. "Look, the blood, there, they were shooting the fucking puppies into the rocks with that thing!"

They'd shot dogs before, for practice or boredom, or because Big Army told them to thin the herd on the outpost, but this was different. The two soldiers getting yelled at had launched several puppies from the slingshot into the mountain while a third young man stood on the small, rocky hillside where the dead animals were lying. He stood to the side of the animals and was there to dash their heads in with a large rock in case they survived the toss.

"Oh, for Christ's sake. You fucking idiots. Clean this shit up and find something to do. We're back on rotation tonight."

"Roger Sarn't," the men said.

The sergeant turned to the soldier who was bothered, "I'm sorry Romo, I know you like the dogs. If I'd known they were doing this, I'd have stopped them. They're fucking stressed out and they're tired, and bored, and scared. Do you understand? They're screwed up because they're so worn the fuck out."

"It's fucked up Sarn't, and it's wrong."

"I'll deal with it. Go square yourself away and start thinking about tomorrow. It'll be a foot patrol."

Private Martinez had been watching the whole thing. He'd filmed it with a little flip camera and later emailed it to the main base where the honchos lived. For a day or two the sergeant was worried about demotion and what that meant but the higher ups on the outpost were able to squash it without anyone getting in any real trouble.

And yet he still rose and ran the dog. He woke the wife, placing a coffee next to where she slept whether on the couch or in the bed.

He got the kids dressed and then left for work, teaching children that didn't really want to be there and rarely listened to him. It was insulting with the things he'd done. There had been enough to make him old. The tiny, whizzing, metal pieces that snapped past his head like angry spirits: they screamed at him and then were gone, furious that he'd been lucky and elusive in those days. Nowadays he wasn't making much of anything, except for money. He wasn't making anything that he could walk home and show those who loved him.

The three men moved quickly up the mountain. Their breathing was strained and their eyes lolled, wide and searching and quick. They followed the blood trail. The man who'd almost killed them with a light machine gun was running, bleeding, his way up the mountain. He no longer had a right hand and there was a hole in the side of his face that gaped open. There were broken teeth and bits of tongue that spilled out. The three Americans moved from boulder to boulder, making themselves tiny behind their rifles as they turned each corner in the creek that ran through boulders and trees, up and down the mountain. They poured up the hillside, advancing from one spot to another, heaving under the armor, moving, liquid and fluid and terrified. The man missing a hand and part of his face and that had tried to kill them kept moving in front of them. The blood pouring out of his wounds into pools on the hillside led the Americans that chased him. From boulder to tree to tiny cave, they leap frogged, rifles at eye level, following the blood. They moved quickly but the man was ahead of them, and wounded, and terrified. He moved at a dead run up the hill. The Americans stopped as the creek bed opened into a rocky plateau. They could no longer see the blood trail and were exhausted and had only a little water. The allied Afghan security guards, led by Lal Abdali, picked up the chase and almost caught the man when his unseen partner put three holes in Lal Abdali's chest. The Afghan security commander bled to death before the bird came to get him. The man whose hand was blown off and whose shattered face bled all over the mountain died in the next village, hideous and white.

It was all okay. Everything was regimented. He knew that time was hurtling forward but that nothing he could do would be new, or different. Not even his specific set of mistakes and accomplishments were new or extraordinary. He was all of those who had already lived.

He continued to shower, dress, and wake the kids. He did it every day. He made breakfast for the kids and then woke up the wife. He laid coffee by her head. He knew these weren't events that happened to him. They were choices. They were the balance due for the other events, the other stones he'd thrown in the pond, ripples returning to shore. Even his kids' choices and consequences were their own. They were only ten he'd say, but that demon goddess Lilith, somewhere in the back of his mind—that Persian bitch! —would tell him that they were guilty too. Old magic, that's what he needed. The good stuff before Christ. The numbers. The horned and winged gods. The blades and statues and Jupiter himself. It was all happening now.

The boy was four. He was happy and ran around the house with all of his friends and his sister's friends. They played with toys and threw balls at one another while his mom's pretty, young friend helped them make little capes out of felt and yarn. After cake they all piled into the tiny backyard. It had rained and the flowers and tree branches drooped in towards all the guests. The deck was raised, seven or eight feet above the ground and below it the grass turned to mud. The boy's father was barefoot and had hung the piñata from the deck. It swung freely, out into the grassy yard and then back under the deck where there was the mud and broken glass from tenants of the house long before the family had moved in. The father was tall, and his feet were muddy. He'd been drinking all day and had set down the vodka to hang the piñata. When he spoke to people he looked past their eyes or at the ground. The last time he tried to speak to someone when he was this drunk, he started crying and it had embarrassed the father and the woman he was talking to.

The kids all piled outside, the rest of the parents coming with them. Some of the parents were nursing beers or drinks and a few of them would head around the side of the little bungalow to smoke without the kids seeing them. The father lined the kids up, encouraged them and, except for a stutter step or two, only his wife knew he'd drank too much. The children filed through the line, taking turns with the piñata. They'd whack at it two or three times but were too small still to do more than make it swing. After a couple go-rounds the father set his drink down, backed the kids up, and pulled a lock-blade knife from his pocket. It was short and thick and sharp, and he jabbed it into the piñata's belly. He stabbed it a couple times and then laughed as he sawed his way from the belly to the neck of the sparkly donkey. He removed the knife, shut it, and put it back into the pocket of his shorts. His son was happy and bashed the donkey three or four more times till the candy spilled out the belly. The parents just looked at him and for the rest of the day would have only the basest conversations with the man. The kids were too young to notice any difference and had fun for the rest of the day.

Later, the man and his wife fought in the kitchen. She threw his phone across the room, shattering it to pieces. The man pushed her to the counter. She slammed her foot against a cupboard, and it bled. The man put on his clothes and shoes and sat waiting for the police to arrive. He waited on the big, deep couch in the living room. He woke up on the couch the next morning realizing he'd been an animal and crawled into bed with his wife. She let him stay there, his arm draped over her. She stared, unspeaking, at the wall in front of her, deciding where the rest of their lives would go.

He woke up and ran the dog and showered. He dressed and woke up the kids. This kept happening. Then he made breakfast for the kids and woke up his wife. This happened every day, too. He made it happen, this routine. He got them ready for school and then left for work, teaching other children that didn't want to learn and didn't listen to what he had to say. His wife took their kids to school. Often, they would fight, his wife and he, over little things that had grown large. These little-things-fought-over masked the cavernous things that would implode the life they led. He tried to leave those things alone. The drink helped too. This all kept happening day in and day out. This was done to throw the tarp over it all, over the real, stinking, fetid mass that was owed to whomever it was that collected what was owed. He desperately tried to settle the bill and keep his life, the good one: the father and husband, the good friend. He tried to keep the good one alive and out there earning for the one who would wind up collecting it all in the end.

DOUBLE†DAGGER

Double Dagger Books is Canada's newest military-focused publisher. Conflict and warfare have shaped human history since before we began to record it. The earliest stories that we know of, passed on as oral tradition, speak of war, and more importantly, the essential elements of the human condition that are revealed under its pressure. We are dedicated to publishing material that, while rooted in conflict, transcend the idea of "war" as merely a genre. Fiction, non- fiction, and stuff that defies categorization, we want to read it all.

Because if you want peace, study war.

www.doubledagger.ca

11 / 3 / 11

A novel

by A E MERRICK

THE TRUTH WILL SET YOU FREE

11/3/11

9/11 was an inside job.

The moon landings were faked.

JFK is alive and well and spends his days with Elvis.

Everyone knows what happened on 11/3/11. But do they really know the truth?

John Doe – JD to his friends – knows for a fact that things are not as they seem. The world is wearing blinders, but he has his eyes wide open. And the more you truly know, the crazier you seem.

Dive into a rabbit hole of conspiracy theories and see the world through JD's eyes. AE Merrick's debut novel is a wild ride through mind control, paranoia, and isolation in search of the ever-elusive truth.

ABOUT THE AUTHOR

A.E. Merrick is a Toronto-based dilettante who has experimented with a number of different identities, occupations, and pastimes. They are uncomfortable with publicly searchable databases of personal information. They write truth rather than fiction. 11/3/11 is their first novel.

INTERDICTION

INTERDICTION

The world of private security is a lucrative one, a collection of corporate armies built to compete in what has become a thirty billion dollar a year industry. Staffed largely by regular military and special forces veterans, these companies provide services to governments and the corporate world.

What would happen if one of the world's most powerful private security firms went rogue?

Daniel Evans has just been sworn in as the 46thPresident of the United States and his first major initiative is to fulfill his biggest campaign promise—the complete withdrawal of all American military personnel from the Middle East.

Nicholas DeGuerra is the CEO of TitanX Security, the world's largest private security company. He's a self-made man, a former Delta operator turned businessman who knows that the new president's policy is a threat to his financial security. He's just launched a desperate operation to save his company and his fortune.

Brian Thompson is a United States Navy Chief nearing retirement and looking forward to life after the military. A staffing shortage puts him onboard USS James E. Williams, an aging destroyer deployed to the Horn of Africa.

When a Pakistani nuke is stolen, the President of the United States sends Thompson and the USS Williams on a last-ditch interdiction mission to intercept the weapon and derail DeGuerra's plan.

ABOUT THE AUTHOR

Matt Hardman is a retired U.S. Navy Chief Petty Officer who currently works as a marine engineering consultant to the Navy's DDG 51 Shipbuilding Program Office. While on active duty, he served onboard a submarine, two aircraft carriers, two amphibious transports, one submarine tender, and one destroyer. During his final tour of duty, he served as the Engineering Department Chief, or "Top Snipe," for the USS James E. Williams (DDG 95). He is also a husband and father of six children and currently resides in Calvert County, Maryland.

ABOUT THE AUTHOR

Christopher Lyke is an American writer and teacher living in Chicago. He served in Afghanistan and Africa as an enlisted infantryman in the U.S. Army. Chris co-founded and edits Line of Advance, a literary blog for veterans, as well as overseeing the annual Colonel Darron L. Wright Memorial Writing Awards.

He can usually be found running with his dog in Logan Square or catching a game at Floyd's Pub. Lyke's work has been featured in such venues as Blaze Vox, Military Experience and the Arts' literary journal As You Were, Heart of a Veteran, Why We Write from Middle West Press, and he won the short story award in Proud To Be: Writing by American Warriors Vol. 4.